**SHORELESS
SKIES**

Designed & Written by
Derek A. Kamal

Illustrations by
Claudia Cangini

Interior Design & Layout by
Jacob Hunt

Playtested by
Jeremy Eric C., Jeremy Hesse, Ian Kelley, Jason Martin, Maciej Matuszewski, Mark Prier, and Matt Spoon

"Mirth" mechanic by
Jeremy Hesse

Inspired by...

Remarkable Inns & Their Drinks by Loresmyth Games

Four Against Darkness by Ganesha Games

Tiny Taverns by Gallant Knight Games

Apocalypse World by Lumpley Games

Copyright © 2022 Shoreless Skies Publishing, LLC
ISBN: 978-0-9972727-9-6

The Broken Cask Society

TABLE OF CONTENTS

INTRODUCTION 1

A BRIEF HISTORY OF THE BROKEN CASK SOCIETY 3
    Notable Members 5
    Structure 8
    The Society House 9
    Your Own Society 10

SOCIETY ORIENTATION 11
    Terms 12
    Gathering Materials 16
    Playbooks 16
    Making Your Own Character 23
    Society Log 25
    Journaling & Narrating 26
    The Random Tables 28
    Tests 28
    Concerning Solitaire Play 31
    Safety, Tone, & Collaboration 31

THE SOCIETY AWAITS	35
Preparation	36
Setting Out	37
Journeying	43
Arrival	49
Feasting	53
Sleep	59
Session End	61
ADVANCED SOCIETY MANUAL	63
Solitaire Options	63
Playing with a GM	64
Society Standings	65
Improvement	66
The Finest Inns	68
REFERENCE	71
Rules Clarification	72
Playbooks	75
Log	79
Standings Board	83
Session Outline	84
Tables	87
BACKERS LIST	129

INTRODUCTION

> *"There are many fine inns here in the wide world. Many disgusting lumps as well. It is for us, the brave of the Society, to search out and find the cream of the crop. No stream shall go unforded, no mountain unclimbed, no ale undrunk.*
>
> *"It is we noble few who suffer the elements and dangers of the road to uphold a noble code: any inn worth of the name must be of the highest quality. And, no last call shall happen before eleven at night!"*
>
> —SOCIETY FOUNDER BONIFACE

WHAT IS THIS GAME?

The Broken Cask Society is a tabletop storytelling game in which you, alone or with amiable companions, traverse the wilds of the world in search of the finest inns, taverns, wineries, alehouses, drinkeries, pubs, cafes, and mead halls. You will use dice, paper, pens, and your imagination to work together and tell stories of your travels and your legendary feasts.

It is a roleplaying game and you will inhabit the role of your Society member, a certifiable specialist in the comestible sciences. However there is no Game Master. You will use random tables and your collective imagination to set the scene and describe what happens next.

This is not a game for those wishing to make strict tactical decisions or engage in fearsome and detailed combat. It is not designed as a space in which to tell excruciating stories of significance nor is it much of a game for character development.

It's a moment to relax in imaginary inns. It's a chance to journey through beautiful landscapes in your mind's eye. It's the means to tell a good, fun story with your friends. Most importantly, it's a game made for you to enjoy.

Is this like the original Broken Cask?

Yes! And no!

The Broken Cask was about operating a fantasy inn. This happened through lots of randomly generated events and actions. This game is about enjoying those inns…through lots of randomly generated events and actions.

So playing the game will feel very similar to Broken Cask: you'll make many die rolls to find out what happens, keep track of your stats, meet lots of interesting characters, and eat delicious food. You'll notice some of the same things as this game is set in the same world and, hopefully, you'll appreciate the same silly and fun tone. You can use some of those tables (such as inn names) from *The Broken Cask* with this game. You might even choose to visit your very own inn!

However, this game is more about journeying, eating, and drinking. And you can do it with friends!

You will gather materials, such as this book, the character playbooks, the random tables, and so on, make your Society members, and be on your way.

But first, you should know a bit about what you're getting yourself into.

a BRIEF HISTORY of the BROKEN CASK SOCIETY

Tens upon tens of years ago, they say our world was polluted with the remains of subpar establishments, mediocre meaderies, and dive bars barely worthy of the name. They say one had to travel far and wide to find a decent pint, and even farther and wider(er?) to find a comfortable seat. For, as we all know, entering into your preferred tavern should be like putting on a night shirt or slipping into a warm bath: luxurious, comfortable, and hopefully cheap.

Alas, such finery was difficult to locate in those days and it was not until the Broken Cask Society carried the standard of hot meal and cold drink in good measure (and of reasonable price) that things took a turn for the better. There is still a long way to go to elevate the inns of the lands, but it is an honorable quest. And we mean to finish it.

Somehow, the story all begins with someone called Boniface.

Notable Members

Society Founder Boniface

A stodgy but fashionable half-ork, Master Boniface grew tired of the solitary tavern in his little home hamlet, that being the now infamous Bright Casket Inn. And so this simple farmer, at the ripe old age of thirty and one winters, sold his turnip fields and bought a walking stick. His travels famously took him all the way across town, two whole blocks, to the Bright Casket. There, they say, he kicked the door off its hinges, apologized because he'd only meant to open it, and demanded the tavern (barely worthy of the title) clean up its act. Now the Bright Casket is a marvel of hospitality and a testimony to what our Founder stands for.

His hometown thus seen to, Boniface trekked over hill and dell, from dive to resplendent country house. When he emerged from his ranging eight years later he imagined a league, a club, a society of the finest tasters and wanderers these lands have ever known. After another year of travels to spread the word and gather the faithful, the Broken Cask Society was born.

Now in his seventieth and one year, Master Boniface serves a more ornamental role. He rarely leaves the Society House, but instead sits by the fire and enjoys tales spun by the more active members while sipping on juniper tea mixed with brandy. It is said that many of his descendents can be found here and there in the world, though he claims none of them.

Boniface enjoys his pet goats and a Sunday stroll from his bedroom to the bathroom.

Society Lead Orsni

The legend of the beard of Orsni precedes her status as the current Society Lead. For, while all dwarves keep beards, it is rare for a female dwarf to keep one of such particular magnificence. Plaited, bound, and conditioned, it drags on the ground if not maintained and, they say, still hides crumbs and stains from her epic tavern crawls. Reports also tell us about one night of especial imbibery, when she confessed to being raised in dirt poverty under some mountain somewhere. As such, the habit of collecting and saving and hoarding has never left her, making her a rather fine choice in leadership.

Orsni keeps the Broken Cask Society organized and motivated. She produces the quarterly newsletter and accepts dues. Mostly she is known around the Society House for rousing songs and tales of adventure and her rare stamp collection.

Bursar Potts

Some have said that in the heat of battle the conscious mind nearly shuts down in a fit of adrenaline and anxiety and one begins to act on instinct. Such instinctual ferocity never made itself apparent in Cordelius Potts, at least not until he began doing accounts. The current Broken Cask Society bursar ensures all dues are tallied and all expenditures are noted. Rarely seen outside his office, this human cares little for appearances and even less for adventure; he's here to make sure you don't accrue more than your fair share of the coffers.

All expenses and monetary request go through him and if you run up a nasty tally you can expect an invoice hastily and angrily. His pet ocelot, Yuki, might even deliver it to you.

Agent Homza

Gorfrier Homza is the chief agent of the Society. Her role is that of publicist, herald, scout, recruiter, and snack-packer. Rarely in one place for more than a single day, this elf rides here and there gathering reconnaissance on new inns and spreading word of the exploits of the Society.

Certainly there are other agents within the Broken Cask Society. Perhaps you wish to become one yourself! But none are as legendarily pennywise and persuasive as Homza. She offers a military background as explication of her skills and physical prowess, but to what military and of what time period remains a shifting fact. One day it's the High Battalion of the Moon the next it's the Subterranean Delver's League. Whatever the case, she is very good at what she does and that includes popping up unexpectedly and unexpectedly caffeinated.

Structure

Apart from the offices previously listed, the Society keeps little by way of formal constitution or charter. Somehow the operation runs smoothly. Those new to the Broken Cask Society are considered initiates and then, after some arbitrary amount of time and the endorsement of a sponsor, they become full members.

No official awards and ceremonies have taken hold in the Society as yet, as the organization is still in a relative infancy among the broader consortiums of the land, but unofficially there is much to discuss.

Those members and initiates of a more sporting disposition keep a running standing of who has gone where and drank what and eaten this or that. It follows that a rather complex algorithm is employed to tabulate who is in the lead, though all agree it is a rather absurd and inefficient means of keeping tab. These standings are updated quarterly but as of now there is little award for being at the top apart from bragging rights.

To that end, there are many friendly (and not so friendly) rivalries within the Society. Perhaps you shall find yourself in one! Just remember to keep it clean and amiable, otherwise you may hear from Orsni.

High days, holidays, and festal seasons are important to the Society. Even days of obscure and marginal spiritual significance are taken as an excuse to jubilate. If any Society member can claim it, or create it, that day is recognized and a meal is slapped together. In some instances this is done respectfully, with local clergy and faithful included, other times it's a shallow and tawdry affair.

It also holds that when an initiate becomes a member there is a celebration, although the proportion of it depends entirely on the initiate themselves. Oftentimes folk arrive at the Society House ready and willing to do whatever is necessary to join the Society, while a select few weedle their way in through the robust (some would say "abusive") intern programme.

Well-liked and promising initiates may have a days-long party with dozens of courses and many celebrants; the more annoying and begrudgingly accepted members (those usually being young know-it-alls and roustabouts) may be attended only by their sponsors and perhaps Boniface if he's bored. It is after this party that initiates receive their membership badge and a small coupon for the gift shop.

The Society House

The home base of the Society is a three story villa in the center of the city. Which city? Why, that's up to you!

Through the main gate is a splendid courtyard that is tended by Three-Heron the gardener and their volunteer sprites. Besides the typical displays of shrub and flower, this courtyard holds many interesting and important ingredients for cooking and brewing.

Inside is a vast and sprawling warren that is part museum, part laboratory, and part dance hall. Many rooms contain trinkets and recollections of the epic pub crawls of the past, from golden stein trophies to jars of dragon's

venom (said to go nicely with mince pie) to a mythical hardened biscuit that refuses to spoil. This is also where copies of the Great Ledger are kept. It is a grand, leather-bound tome that indexes only the finest inns of the land as submitted by Society members and approved by Boniface himself.

In the distillery, Society elites work day and night to perfect the art of spirits. The brewery smells of yeast and hops at all hours, as the more adventuresome sorts take turns beguiling the world with their concoctions after hearty rounds of testing. The kitchens hum from morning to night and the heat of the ovens and stoves are constantly fed by unpaid interns and welcomed vagrants. The results of these culinary experiments are either exquisite or deadly. The details of most can be found in the periodical publication *Annals of Kentu*.

In short, the Broken Cask Society house is a place to begin a journey, to poke around, to rest, and to freely engage the most pleasing pastime of all: food and drink.

Your Own Society

All of the above is here to get your imagination going and to help you shape your character. However you wish to tweak and prod the Society, what it is and what it does, is up to you and your table. Do not take this chapter as set-in-stone.

SOCIETY ORIENTATION

While we are all ready to face the road and enjoy the offerings of the great inns of the land, there are a few things to get out of the way first. As an initiate, we recommend you read this society manual at least one time thoroughly so you understand the basics.

These include the essential rules of the game, character creation, the general tone of a session, and the terms we use to play. Let's begin with those.

Terms

1d6 – a standard six-sided die. You will use this for every test and roll.

1d3 – a three-sided die. You may use a d6, but ⚀ becomes 1, ⚁ becomes 2, and ⚂ becomes 3

2d6 – Roll two six-sided dice (or 1d6 twice) and total the results.

d66 – Roll 2d6 to generate a two-digit number. The first roll is the tens place, the second is the ones. So ⚃⚁ would be 42.

Advantage – Roll twice and keep the better result

Disadvantage – Roll twice and keep the worse result. This will normally be a lower number, if you're rolling to resolve an event. If it is disadvantage when rolling on a table, choose the more challenging or uncomfortable result.

Ensorceled – Some spell or other has cursed you! Take Disadvantage on all tests until is removed or you rest at an Inn. Optionally, a party member may take disadvantage on any test instead of the Ensorceled character (representing the Ensorceled character interfering with their test in some way).

Event – Any time you generate a random activity it's referred to as an event. Sometimes you will test, sometimes you will not. In essence, an event is something the game world does to you, while a move is something you do to the game.

Exhausted – When you become exhausted, unless otherwise instructed, choose one stat (B, M, or H) and cross it out. You automatically fail any tests using that stat until you Rest at an inn or until some other game effect revives you.

If you become exhausted because of Morale loss, you may restore +3 Morale after crossing out the stat.

If all three of your stats become Exhausted, immediately skip ahead to the Rest phase and then narrate how you got there.

SOCIETY ORIENTATION

Flip – Literally flip your die from one side to the opposite side. So ⚀↔⚅ ⚁↔⚄ ⚂↔⚃. Sometimes this listed before a test difficulty (eg "Flip H1"); this means you flip your result when you test.

Forward – Anytime a notation says "+1 that forward" you add 1 the next time you test for that. For example: "+1 Adventure forward" means you will add 1 the next time you test during on an Adventure. "+1M forward" means you add 1 next time you test using Mind. If there is no modifier and it simply says "+1 forward" add 1 to the very next test. And, yes, this can stack so you make take X forward multiple times!

However this mostly applies to test rolls. In the case of +1 forward when rolling on a table, it will always be specifically noted. For example, "+1 next time you roll for a Journey event" or "+1 next time you roll on the Arrival table."

Gear – This is the stuff you bring with you as you travel: sleeping bags, walking sticks, granola, a good bit of rope. Start by checking all those boxes.

"Spending" it means erasing a check. If you see +1 Gear, that should be read as "restore 1 Gear" by checking the box if possible. "Add +1 Gear box" means you actually draw another box on your playbook, as you are now able to carry more gear for one reason or another.

Hit – A successful test. Your total roll after modifiers met or exceeded the target.

Improve – To level up. Games lasting more than one session may wish to expand their play by using the improve rule to enhance their characters. More on that later.

Mirth – Travel, good food, and good friends, are what the Society is all about. These things are worth working for because of how they make us feel! Mirth is that tingling you get when things are going your way. This currency can be spent to trigger basic moves. You can tick Mirth boxes on your sheet or use tokens of your choosing.

Miss – A failed roll; your total was less than the target.

Morale – This is a general abstraction of how you are doing. You can lose Morale from a tiring journey, from eating or drinking too much, from that feeling of disappointment that comes with a bad meal. Start the session by checking all solid Morale boxes on your playbook. When you lose morale you erase one of those boxes. If all your Morale is gone you become Exhausted.

"+1 Morale" means you regain one point of morale and can check a box. It does not mean you gain an extra morale box. Unless otherwise stated you cannot have more morale than you have maximum boxes.

Moves – On your playbook is a set of basic moves and and moves specific to your character. Moves are generally actions your character takes that require a roll. These are explained more later.

Narrate – Just like it sounds! Whenever you take the lead and tell the story, you are narrating.

"Or…" – Many events will use the word "or" when you resolve. If it does not say to choose then the first thing listed must be done if possible. If that is not possible, the "or" kicks in and you do the next thing. For example, "Remove 1 item, or take -1M forward" means you must try and remove an item first. If you have no items to remove, then you take the -1M forward.

Ongoing – The effect continues, affecting all tests, until it is resolved in some way, typically by resting at an inn.

Phase – As a GM-less game, Broken Cask Society follows a fairly strict outline to provide structure for the players. The main steps of play are referred to as phases and they are Prepare, Journey, Arrive, Feast, and Rest.

Poison – When you are poisoned, you are not feeling well. This may not literally be poison. If you roll a 1 on any test the poison kicks in and you become Sick.

Roll – If a table instructs you to simply "roll" that means you should roll 1d6 and follow what happens next. There are no effects or modifiers.

"Roll on…" – Typically when the game says to roll, it refers to you acting to resolve an event as described. If the effect pertains to a random table, it should always say "when you roll on a table" or "when you roll on this table" to make it clear that the effect is meant for a random table and not your character's action.

SOCIETY ORIENTATION

Sick – When you are Sick you suffer -1 ongoing to all tests until you are cured or you rest at an inn.

Society – Why, the Broken Cask Society, of course! A league of adventuresome gourmands and intrepid imbibers who journey here and there in search of the finest inns in the land.

"Take Note" – If a table tells you to "take note," it means to summarize the result in the correct section of your playbook and then try to reintroduce it to the narrative at a later time when it may apply to a test or other event. When you do so, erase the note.

If it was negative, take disadvantage forward and then mark XP; if it was positive, take advantage forward. You can use this effect on a test, table roll, or move. You may even use it on another player's test if they agree.

Test – Whenever a Test is mentioned this refers to some happening a player must roll to resolve using their B/M/H stats. See the rules for action resolution above.

Traits – Traits are overt pieces of your personality and background. You start with two and may invoke them with the basic move Expertise. You narrate how they help you in a particular situation, after a test, to reroll.

XP – Experience points. When you are told to "mark XP," check one of your XP boxes. A full bar can be spent to improve your character at the end of session. Most often you will mark XP when you miss a test.

Gathering Materials

To play the game you will need a few different things, either on a screen or on your table. They are presented in this book (most especially in the Reference section), but you are encouraged to download the play kit from ShorelessSkies.com for an extra copy.

Take a moment to gather the Society Log, playbooks, a few pencils with an eraser, at least one six-sided die, the random tables, and a blank playbook if you are making your own character.

Playbooks

The Broken Cask Society utilizes playbooks to represent and keep track of your character. There are five playbooks for you to choose from, each its own template for your Society member. It's the drawing; you get to color it by choosing your heritage, history appearance, and anything else that breaths life into your character.

The playbooks are described in brief below and presented in full in the reference chapter (as well as the downloadable play kit).

When it is time to create your character, choose the playbook that sounds most appealing and try not pick a duplicate that someone else at the table has chosen. If you do, it's okay — there will be enough to distinguish one from another, especially by picking different moves.

Within the rules of the game, moves are the main way one develops their character and takes unique actions. All characters have access to the basic moves, but then there is a set of moves specific to your playbook that align with your characters special abilities and training. There is also a move that's already been selected for you — this negative move is a kind of character quirk meant to get you into trouble!

After making your selection, check all applicable boxes as the playbook instructs you to. Take some time to think about your character. Jot down ideas you have about where they come from, what they like, why they are a part of the Society, and why they are on these journeys. This will help you to narrate and further color your stories as you go.

The Campaigner

Hardy, tough, fun-loving. The Campaigner has seen a thing or two in their day, probably during military service, and are used to roughing it. They are difficult to daunt or exhaust but they are quick-tempered.

Choose the Campaigner if you enjoy a physically tough sort of character who isn't particular about what they eat; they're just happy to be here.

The Vintner

These folks are all about wine and the lifestyle that comes with it. Much of their time is spent savoring and learning about new sorts of vino, and so they have a rather academic and erudite manner about them. With such a manner comes a certain air of pretention and that is a sword with two edges, for some times it helps and some times it hurts.

If you're here to learn more and show off a little bit, the Vintner may be for you.

SOCIETY ORIENTATION

The Pilgrim

The Broken Cask Society is about two things: journeying and eating. The Pilgrim is more focused on the former. Perhaps because of previous employment or a wayward disposition, the Pilgrim has traveled far and wide and knows how to survive in the wild.

If the traveling aspect of the game is a little more appealing than the wining and dining, consider playing the Pilgrim.

The Kegmaster

What can you mix together without an explosion? That is what the Kegmaster wants to know. Part brewer, part alchemist, all fascination, these specialists want to know what's in that concoction and how it got there!

If you like beer or potions or both,
the Kegmaster is for you.

The Gourmand

It's truly a wonder how the many people of the world take fresh ingredients and make them into something special. The Gourmand is both a student of the wonder and a clever hand at it themselves. Perhaps they are simply here to explore the many flavors on offer or perhaps they want to learn how to make it themselves.

The Gourmand is all about the food.

Making Your Own Character

The Playbooks are there for those who enjoy a simplified character creation process and want to jump into the game as quickly as possible. Experienced players, or those who enjoy a lot of customization, can take a blank character sheet and generate their own.

Name, heritage, and appearance are pretty straightforward. As they have no real effect on the game rules you can do as you please. You can also use the random tables in the reference section of this book to generate a name and heritage, as well as quirks and other characteristics.

Use the following rules for the rest of your character.

Traits

You need at least one personality trait and one background trait. Personality traits are just those: singular descriptors about your character's attitude or disposition, something that you can "cash in" to use points of Mirth for rerolls. It should be simple, balanced, and realistic. So "Irresistibly Charming" would not be a good personality trait as it is too broad and too applicable to too many situations. Simply saying that your character is "charming" is enough to go with because it leaves room for failure.

Here are some more basic examples:
- Agreeable
- Brave
- Conversationalist
- Easily Amused
- Lone Wolf
- Old Fashioned
- Thoughtful
- Tidy

Background traits reflect your personal history. It could be a job you had before you joined the Society or a place you grew up or your relation to a family member. Imagine who you your character is and why they are a part of the Broken Cask Society, and go from there.

Examples could include:
- Agricultural Upbringing
- Former bandit
- Grew up on the streets
- Good family life
- Minor royalty
- Orphan
- Religious upbringing
- Scholar
- Tragic Past
- Well-traveled

Stats

The statistics of your character are numerical representations of their capabilities in any given situation. They are represented in three broad categories.

Body is the physical prowess of the character. A high ranking in Body could mean uncommon endurance, great strength or agility, any sort of physicality that could help carry them through a difficult moment.

Mind is the general intellect and wisdom. A low Mind ranking would be a character who is perhaps more intuitive than analytical; not a natural problem solver.

Heart represents social intelligence and compassion. A high score in Heart is the type of character who knows how to relate to people and show empathy.

You should randomly generate your rating for each statistic by rolling 1d6 and then using the following:

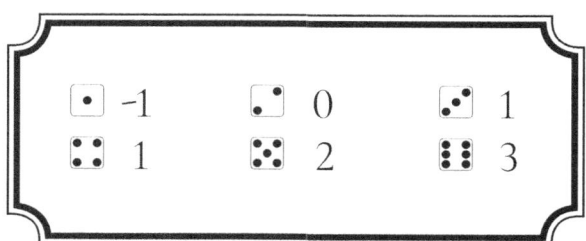

Moves

All characters can act on any test utilizing their stats, as will be explained later. All characters can utilize basic moves. But what makes one character different from another is the special moves that they can make. The pre-written playbooks have some examples to use as a template. **You should build off of these and generate at least one of your own character moves.**

Taking +1 in a specific situation is an easy go-to, as is making a difficulty 3 test to gain some other bonus.

You must also create one move with a negative effect. This is some difficulty inherent to your character by way of their experience, training, or personality. Maybe you have a short attention span or your experience with childhood bullies means you cannot resist a fight. It should be a penalty that triggers in a specific situation and it should be balanced against the existing moves.

A -1 penalty is a simple enough option, as is taking disadvantage. Use the existing ones as a template and create your own.

Society Log

On each playbook is a section for the player to keep up with their exploits. This includes items you pickup along the way and conditions that affect you when you test. These thing are meant for your character only.

There is also a log pertaining to your travels in which to take more detailed notes. This can be helpful when playing more than one session and keeping track of things that affect the whole party, or just to have a record of your days.

This is your Society Log in which you chronicle your journeys and the inns you have raided. Most of this log exists for the simple purpose of notation and documentation. It's helpful to take even brief notes to help you remember what is going on and which characters you have come across.

With regards to the rules of the game, however, it is rather important that you keep track of how many successes you have when you journey along with the prestige level of the inns you are visiting, not to mention

your successes at the feast table. This will all be explained later and in excruciating detail, but do keep it in mind.

Journaling & Narrating

As a game for both single players and groups there is a great variability one can take when approaching a session of *The Broken Cask Society*. Some players will enjoy a bare bones approach by rolling and ticking boxes while others will go deep into their singular or collective imaginations, a theater of the mind approach if you like, and flesh out entire worlds and characters.

If you are playing on your own, consider writing out your events on the Society Log, or keeping a journal.

If you are playing in a group, everyone must narrate and work together to tell the story.

"What do you do?"

Oftentimes, and especially when using the random tables, the question will be posed in various forms: what do you do? How do you handle this?

Even when not plainly stated, this is assumed. You are going to do something about the situation. Any good GM will ask this question a dozen times during the course of a game session and that's what the game is doing for you, prompting you to join in the story and play your part.

Whether alone or with fellow Society members, take a moment and tap into your imagination. What would your character do? How does it fit in this story and this game?

Such confines are equally beneficial and frustrating: you cannot pick up an axe and murder the bard for breaking a string, nor can you do nothing. So challenge yourself to come up with a response that is fitting and, hopefully, entertaining.

Moreover, it is hoped that the dice are on your side and that what you do succeeds. But don't forget, losing is fun!

The Random Tables

A big part of the game, especially as there is no Game Master, is utilizing the random tables to inspire the beats of your story. There are quite a few of these tables and they are included in the back of this book. How you use them is up to you! You can stick with the book, print them out, use the pdf on a laptop or tablet, or try the app! All of this can be found at ShorelessSkies.com.

These tables are used in a fairly straightforward fashion. They will tell you what dice to roll (1d6, 2d6, or d66) and then give you some kind of prompt. It is then up to you to describe, either to yourself or to the others you are playing with, what happens and how your character reacts. As stated above, "What do you do?" Then you will roll to see how your character does and follow what the table says if you hit or miss.

This is how your stories are told.

Some are described as being optional in the rules and marked with an asterisk in the text. These optional tables are there to help you flesh out your stories and generate plot action, but they are not necessary. If you are pressed for time, or simply want a more straightforward game, you may skip these.

You test to find out what happens and the majority of playbook moves modify what happens when you test. So how does that work?

Tests

Well! You will do a great many things during your travels: face the dangers of the road; enjoy exotic dishes; sup new and strange brews. When the time comes to see how your character does with, say, that odd new ale or the crocodile standing between them and the next leg of the journey, we test. A test is a simple roll of the die, the most gamey bit of the game. This is sometimes referred to as "action resolution."

The random tables will prompt you with a situation and a notation. Some of your playbook moves will do the same. This will almost always be represented by a letter and a number. The letter is **B** for Body, **M** for Mind, or **H** for Heart, described in the stats section above. The number

SOCIETY ORIENTATION

is the target you must reach when rolling dice and adding bonuses, so the target will look something like "B3" or "H2."

If your roll total equals that number, or is higher than the number, you hit and succeed. If not, you miss. In both instances the table or move will tell you what happens, you narrate, notate, and carry on.

To resolve a test, take a look at your playbook. What is the rating for the stat in question? Next, see if you have any conditions that apply, such as Disadvantage or +1 forward.

With those firmly in mind, roll 1d6. Add or subtract your stat and conditions to create a total. If your total is that target number or higher, you did the thing. Otherwise you did not. Now do what the words say to do.

Basic Moves

You may also choose to spend Mirth to influence your roll. Mirth is the currency that you spend to access the basic moves. The term "basic" is there to signify that all characters can use these moves, regardless of playbook. They are as follows and each costs you one point of Mirth.

Expertise – Invoke a trait to reroll after a test. If that die did not do what you wanted it to do, spend one point of Mirth and then pick one of your traits. Narrate to explain how this trait helps you to recover after your flub and reroll the die.

> *Wulflen is a Gourmand with the Thoughtful personality trait. After missing a test to communicate with a local, she pauses, notes she has 1 Mirth and decides to spend it by saying, "I'm a rather thoughtful person, so considering that what I just said didn't hit I think I'm able to correct the situation." Spending Mirth and invoking the trait lets her use the Expertise move to reroll.*

Consideration – Take +1 before you test. If you spend a moment to think about what's going on and how you're going to handle it, you will almost always do better. That's what this is.

Inspiration – Invoke a trait to make a playbook move as if it was a hit without rolling. Most playbook moves require you to test and hit for maximum effect — a moment of inspiration means you can do great things without the extra effort! You just have to be able to explain how one of your traits allows you to do this.

Fast-talk – Flip your die after a test. "So, what had happened was..." After a test you can improve your roll with a quick word and a point of Mirth. This means you can take your die and flip it to the exact opposite side, assuming that would be beneficial. It's kind of like a reroll but you know what you're getting.

Take Action – If you want your character to do something that you can take advantage of later on in the session, you are taking action. Spend a point of Mirth and then explain how your character is preparing or otherwise creating an advantage, then jot it down in the "Take Note" section of your playbook. Go back and read the rules about how this works in the glossary if you need a refresher.

You then spend this to take advantage at an appropriate time when you roll for a test, table roll, or move. Examples include:
- The Vintner reads a horror novel about inns with bedbugs to mentally prepare in case their next Rest might be rough.
- The Pilgrim marks their trail in the woods in case the next day's adventure does not go their way.
- The Campaigner skips breakfast to save room for their next meal.

Resolving a Test

Once the test is complete and you've hit or miss, with or without using your moves, the table tells you what happens. But that's just a sketch! It's up to you to fill in the blanks and describe what happens. Think about what your character did and why they might have succeeded or failed. Consider what is appropriate but, more importantly, consider what would make the story great. How does this action perhaps connect to other moments in the story? Things like that. This is where note taking comes into play.

Let's look at an example roll:

> *Wulflen is having a wild, enjoyable feast at The Stubborn Stable saloon and soapery. During the feast phase of the game, she rolls d66 on the ales table and produce a 26. This is the famous Shinsong River wheat beer, which is marked as H3. This means Wulflen will make a roll using her Heart stat and must total a 3 or higher — truly a formidable drink! Looking over her playbook, Wulflen sees that she get to take +1H forward*

due to a rather heroic moment back on the road and that is well, because her actual Heart stat is a big fat 0. So she rolls 1d6 and the die shows a 4, for a grand total of 5. A hit!

In some cases the table will tell you what happens on a Hit, but during this feasting phase a hit simply means you enjoy the course and mark a point of Mirth on your playbook and that is what Wulflen does.

CONCERNING SOLITAIRE PLAY

The Broken Cask Society has been designed for both cooperative and solo play, but there is always some inherent balancing issues in this regard. What do I mean? Well, playing in a group is such that, yes, there are more rolls and so more can occur, but you still have more bodies (and, importantly, their stats) to deal with the events that come up.

While the game is as balanced as it can be, if you find playing solo to be a bit frustrating then flip to the Reference section for some options that may make your life easier.

SAFETY, TONE, & COLLABORATION

If you are playing *The Broken Cask Society* with friends, take the time to discuss what kind of stories you want to tell and what you're going to do to make sure everyone feels safe during the game. There might be fights, so think about how violent your stories will be. You're headed to a tavern, after all, so there will be alcoholic beverages. Maybe somebody in the group isn't cool with that, so you should stick to soft drinks.

This is a lighthearted and downright silly game meant to evoke a cozy, fantasy atmosphere. Imagine your favorite pub scene from *The Lord of the Rings* or some time spent at the Stardrop Saloon in *Stardew Valley*. Consider the gentle lighting, the wooden accoutrement, the soft din of chatter, the descriptions of luscious food and drink. That's the feeling this game hopes to recreate.

Even in a slice-of-life setting certain types of content can still pop up unexpectedly and spoil the mood, however, so it is important to have some kind of stop in place. This is especially important since there is no

GM. Below is described the perennial "X card" rules but you may use any safety feature you find most useful.

The X Card

Before you begin your game, find a piece of paper or index card and draw a big, fat X on it. Place it in the center of the tabletop. If you are playing online, most virtual tabletops have some kind of feature to let you import safety features or you can simply draw the X using a pen tool.

Should something come up that makes a player uncomfortable or downright triggered, they need only point to the X. This will indicate to the others that play should stop, the story be rewound, and the unsafe moment be redone.

It's important, even when playing with new friends, to respect everyone's use of the safety tool, even if you don't understand their reasoning. In other words, just be cool.

Concerning Combat

There are some combat scenes in *The Broken Cask Society*. These are limited to bar fights and run-ins with bandits or wild beasts on the road. There are no special combat rules.

The table prompts are intentionally vague so you can resolve combat in whatever way suits your group. Some groups may prefer a bloody outcome, while others may describe avoiding danger stealthily or with charisma. Again, take the time to talk with your party (and yourself) about what kind of story you are telling here and act accordingly.

Collaboration

Without a GM to serve as referee, it can be difficult to ensure the game runs smoothly and that all players are included. Most groups will work this out naturally and, typically, one player will step in to help facilitate the game. There are also rules to play with a GM in the reference section of this book.

SOCIETY ORIENTATION

But, remember these hints as you play *The Broken Cask Society* together.

When you are narrating...
- Tell what your character is doing, saying, thinking feeling
- Ask for suggestions if you're stuck
- Describe what's going on in the tavern, or whatever setting you're currently inhabiting
- Take control of and speak for non-player characters
- Take actions (even without a roll) that work towards meeting your goal
- Set something up for the next player
- Do not take control of another player character without permission
- Do not attempt to resolve a scene all on your own.
- Do not make a huge setting change without group consensus.
- Do not keep control of the story longer than you should
- Do not worry about "correct" setting details

When someone else is narrating...
- Ask questions and make suggestions
- Provide setting information or remind them of something that happened earlier
- Jump in as an NPC, respectfully
- Do not overrun the narrator

If you are ever in doubt of what to do next, do what serves the story and is fun. The tables and the rules will guide you, but ultimately it's your game to enjoy!

THE SOCIETY AWAITS

> Well, initiate, you've got rules in your brain and a table full of papers and an imagination loaded with cozy, fantasy imagery. It's time to begin your first journey with the Society!

It is recommended that you have a copy of the session outline with you as you play. This is in the Reference section of this book on and is included in the play kit. Without a GM, the game is set in a fairly strict structure and should be followed as closely as possible.

This chapter takes you through the phases of a session of play and will refer to the outline, along with many of the random tables listed in the reference section as well. More depth and explanation is applied here to help you get a better understanding of how this game works. Narrative prompts are written with a gray highlight. These are the moments where you will pause and, either in your imagination or with your group, narrate the story as it happens.

It is recommended you put a bookmark in the reference section so you can easily flip over there to look at the described tables. Remember that all tables marked with an asterisk are optional.

Samples of play are italicized for your convenience.

Preparation

It takes a lot of planning and thought to strike out upon the road and begin your travels under the standard of the Broken Cask Society. Best to get ready!

Start by preparing your playbook. Your characters should already be made, so as the outline says fill up your morale and gear boxes. If you are continuing a session, review your log to refresh your memory of adventures past. Note how much Mirth, Morale, Gear, and XP has carried over from the last game.

Once per session you *may* choose a Preparation move from that table.

If this is your first session, consider the following questions:
Who are you?
Why are you a part of this Society?

These questions are very important if you are playing in a group. This is the point at which you introduce your character to the world! Imagine the opening scene of your favorite movie, or the introductory chapter of a great novel. How do you want us to meet your Society member?

Then, on all sessions ask:
How are you getting ready to leave?

Perhaps you are saying goodbyes to your loved ones, perhaps you are packing away your lucky hare's foot, or offering farewells to the keg you keep in your cellar. However you do it, this is the time to describe your preparations.

> *Ordissa, Wulflen, and Maurine prepare to set out from the Broken Cask Society house for a grand venture celebrating the turn of fall to winter. This is their second journey together so no introductions are needed. They have agreed to meet at the Society house bright and early, plot out their route, and then be on their way before lunch.*
>
> *They each have gotten their playbooks ready by marking all their Morale and Gear. The characters themselves were already made with Ordissa being a Pilgrim, Wulflen a Gourmand, and Maurine a Vintner. Before heading to the Society house, Wulflen looks at the Preparation table and chooses to take some extra time to celebrate before she goes.*

"Last night," she says, "I had my cousins over for a fine, auroch pie and a glass. It got me in just the right mood to set out."

Then she marks a point of Mirth for her preparation.

Once the others have narrated their preparations it's time to Set Out!

> Any steps in a phase can be rearranged to suit the narrative. Do not feel like you have to do them in the exact order!

Setting Out

All Society expeditions begin at the Society House. Described above, this is a comfortable estate lodged in one of the great cities of the world, described briefly in the chapter concerning the Society's history.

The details surrounding the House are up to you or your group. Which town is it in and why? Who do you know there? Who else is getting ready? These are all things to consider as you weave your first story. Then narrate accordingly.

How do you all know each other?
Is there a reason you are traveling together?
What is the Society House like?
Or are you setting out alone?
If so, why?

Maurine is first to the Society house, so she takes the lead in describing it to the rest of the group. She says, "It's early so there aren't too many members about, but an eager goblin intern offers me some coffee which I take."

Ordissa has an idea and chimes in with a reference to their first session: "That's Carolton's brother!"

Maurine goes along with it. "Oh, right! So we have a nice little conversation before I break away and go to the map room. So whenever you guys arrive I'm poring over this map, trying to plot our course, and shooing away other Society members who want to make small talk."

Departure Event

Optionally, you may roll on the departure events table to see if anything interesting happens before you leave. These events are generally beneficial and can help create fun wrinkles to your characters and their stories. You may roll on the table before or after generating your inn (described in the next phase).

Wulfen steps in to narrate once Maurine finishes. "I come in with a big ol' bag on and sigh when I drop it down: plunk!"

Maurine says, "Ehm, everything alright, Wulflen?"

"Yup! I wipe my forehead and ask where we're going."

"Well!" Maurine continues, picking up some dice. "I've heard about this particular inn that would be perfect for us. We've got this little tradition of ours, traveling between seasons, and I want to make sure we head somewhere special."

Wulflen nods and, realizing Ordissa hasn't spoken up for a while, she says, in character to Maurine, "Where's Ordissa, by the way?"

Maurine shrugs and Ordissa rolls 1d6, looking at the table to find her Departure Event. The others opt to skip theirs. Ordissa says, "I rush in hastily with lots of apologies, like, 'Sorry guys! Sorry! I got caught up. It was the strangest thing. On my way over here my auntie found me on the street to wish me well. Anyways, I'm here now. Where are we going?'"

Ordissa's roll on the Departure Event table produced a 1, which says a loved one offers their blessing before departure and gives you +1 point of Mirth. She marks her playbook accordingly.

> **CONCERNING RIVALS**
>
> There are only a few results that will bring your "Society Rival" into play. One will be mentioned in the example game we have dispersed throughout this chapter. A rival is just that — someone you are competing against within the Society to see who is the bravest and most traveled. Maybe you want to be in this rivalry, or maybe they just keep bugging you for some reason. You can create this rival on the fly or take some time to create them now, either by jotting down a few notes or rolling on the character tables in the back.

Inn Creation

All journeys must have a goal, must they not? This book has three example inns for you to use in the reference section, but most often you will find your destination at random. The suspense!

When the time comes you will use the random tables in the reference chapter of this book (or in the downloadable play kit) to create new inns. Start by finding out the name of where you are headed and then consider the following and narrate:

> *How do you know about this inn?*
> *What have you heard?*
> *What's leading you there?*

"Now that we're all assembled!" says Maurine with a sneering look at Ordissa, "I was just saying how there's a special inn for us to visit together." She puts her hand to her mouth conspiratorially. "I also want to get there before Carolton. He's such a braggart. Anyways..."

Maurine picks up the dice and rolls d66 twice, producing a 35 and a 42. She looks at the inn naming table and says, "The Buzzing Elf is supposed to be very good this time of year, so I was just checking the map to figure out...like, where it is?"

While the others take a moment to think, Maurine fills out the Society Log to keep track of the inn and its location.

Location

You will then roll 2d6 to discover where building itself sits. This could be somewhere quite plain, like a peaceful countryside, or it could be somewhere more exotic like, say, on top of a buried giant.

Create a locale or roll and write it down!

Optionally, you may find news about what's going on in that part of the world. Roll 2d6 again to discover what that location is like. This descriptor is purely for narrative purposes. It will help pad your stories and give your imagination some fuel. In addition to this descriptor, it is good to know what the inn looks like...but that will come later.

> *Maurine decides to knock out a few rolls at once. She picks up the dice again and rolls 2d6 on the location table, then 1d6 on the terrain table, and once more on the days of travel table. "I'm told it's near a magical place in the forest. Should take us two days, give or take. The woods are to the north." She makes that last bit up. "Do either of you know about that place?"*
>
> *Wulflen speaks up in a very intern-ish voice. "That intern hears you and he pops his head in. 'Oh that forest north of this city? The...'" Wulflen looks around for help.*
>
> *"Thornybrook Forest," says Ordissa with a shrug.*
>
> *Wulflen smiles and keeps narrating. "Thank you. 'The Thornybrook Forest?' says the little intern. 'That place is very mysterious. Purple trees, blue moss and the like. Very scary.' Then he produces a tray from nowhere. 'Tea?'"*
>
> *Maurine sips an invisible cup and says, "I take the tea without thinking about it and I say, 'Sounds fun! Are we ready then?'"*

Journeying

Bags packed, characters introduced, maps analyzed, it is time to hit the road! In this phase of *The Broken Cask Society* you will find out what happens on your travels and narrate your journey.

Duration & Terrain

The first step in plotting out a successful journey is to find out how long it is going to take. Roll on the Days of Travel table to plot your timetable. This is important and must be written down, for each day brings a new adventure!

You will also need to know the terrain. Roll 1d6 to uncover the type of land you will need to traverse. This is also important, because each biome has its own set of challenges for you to overcome and will determine which table you will use to create adventures.

As in the above example, one player may roll in quick succession to discover these, or you can take your time.

Optionally you may roll again to find a descriptor about this landscape to influence your narrative. Then take a moment to narrate what's going on during your first day of travel with new adventures and fine food ahead!

> *What are you doing?*
> *What do you see?*
> *What is the weather like?*

"That's a Lot of Tables!"

Some folks enjoy lots of random rolls and some like to get on with it. If you're of the latter kind, make sure you pay attention to which tables are marked with an asterisk. These are optional and only there to help inspire your stories. You can also skip the whole inn and journey creation process by using some of the prewritten Finest Inns in the appendix. You can also head to ShorelessSkies.com to find a the Great Ledger of Inns made by players like you!

Adventures

Every day of your travels means something new is happening! This is called and Adventure and is created randomly using the appropriate tables. Once an event is generated you will narrate and test to find out what happens.

To start, locate the random table that matches the terrain you rolled in the step before this one. Then roll 2d6, total it, and check the table. This is today's adventure!

Each table entry offers you a prompt, but it's up to you to narrate what happens and how your character reacts. Take a moment to flip to one of those tables in the back. I'll wait here.

You'll see examples, such as number 6 on the Forest table, where a treant emerges for some polite conversation or more dangerous adventures like number 11 on the Plains table — a terrible thunderstorm!

What's happened?
What do you do?

You then test to see if what your character does resolves the situation or not using the rules on rolling dice back on page 28.

Whether you hit or miss, the table will tell you what happens but, once again, it's only a prompt; you have to tell the story. Note any mechanical effects (such as +1 forward) that occur on your playbook but then think about why this happened and what your character therefore does.

Finally, mark that day's adventure with a ✓ or ✗ on the Log to show that it was a success or failure. Long days on the road take a toll and it's important to note what's happened so we can find out how you're doing at journey's end!

In between traveling days (and, thusly, adventures) it may be pleasant and wise to describe how you or your crew camps out for the night. But that is strictly optional.

Now let's check back in with our crew.

> *The players know that a two day journey means two Adventures unless some extenuating circumstances pop up. Since Maurine did all the rolls during the last phase, Ordissa offers to take the lead. She grabs the Society Log and starts narrating.*

"We set out earlier than we expected, so it's a nice cool morning as we leave the Society house and pass through the gates of town. I'm singing a marching song almost immediately and I take a swig from the flask Orsni gave me last time."

Wulflen raises her eyebrows. "Oh my."

Ordissa smiles and says, "Want some? It's lemonade."

Wulflen frowns. "Ew."

"Anyways," says Ordissa. "What are you doing, Maurine?"

"Just smiling, taking in the sights, admiring the grassy fields and the warm sunshine before that forest up ahead spoils our day."

"I think it will be okay," says Ordissa. She picks up 1d6 and rolls to find out when the first adventure will be. "So late morning, not long after we set out, something happens."

"Oh boy," says Wulflen.

Ordissa rolls 2d6, adding them together to produce a 6. Then she flips to the Forest table and reads the event prompt: "'A Giant Treant emerges, looking for friends. What do you say?' So I think that we get to the edge of this crazy purple wood and I'm like, 'Deep breath. You guys ready? Let's go!' And then as soon as I say that a pine starts to move suddenly and there's a massive tree person in front of us saying, 'Oh hi!'"

Maurine jump at the opportunity to act in character. "Oh hi there...Mister Tree!"

Ordissa takes on the role of the treant. "Man it's good to see you guys. Haven't had any passers by in like a week! You guys like card games?"

Wulflen steps in now, saying out of character, "Okay we got an inn to visit and I don't think we have time to chat with this dude. What's the test? H3? Okay my Heart is +1 so I think I got this. And I have the point of Mirth from earlier. I say, 'Good Mister Tree, sir, we dearly love card games but we gotta get going. Can we spend some time together on the way back? We mean to return day after tomorrow.'"

All the players could act in this instance, but as she says, Wulflen is best positioned to take the lead. Wulflen then rolls 1d6 and adds her Heart rating. She rolls a 5, plus 1 is six. A hit! Wulflen reads from the table. "'They offer to show you a shortcut. Any player may spend 1 Gear to move to Journey's End now!'"

As the official treant actor, Ordissa says, "That sounds great! Wowee! Thanks! How about I show you a shortcut so you can get back quicker?"

Out of character, the players talk for a second and they agree: while it would be possible to split the group, they don't want to do that; and while the second adventure could lead them to something cool, it could also be risky.

Wulflen says, in character, "Mister Tree, that sounds like a real nice thing. Please show us the way!"

Ordissa marks their one and only adventure as a success with a ✓ the log. Everyone removes 1 Gear from their playbooks by erasing a checkmark. This indicates that they had to spend some of their stuff (rations, maybe some rope or the like) to stay on their feet for the abridged journey. Treants do go fast, after all!

Then Ordissa narrates again. "This treant is super nice but chatty. They won't stop going on about their relations and just when I think I can't take it anymore we are **suddenly clear of the blue wood and there's a town before us and, within, the Buzzing Elf Inn.**"

Journey's End

Once you have completed all Adventures (again, 1 per day of journeying) and narrated your course, your destination is in sight! But first, it's time to calculate the effect the road has had on you.

Start by looking at the results of this journey and totaling all the adventures you've had: +1 for any successes (hit rolls) and -1 for any failure (missed rolls). This total is now your modifier.

If things are looking grim (as in a negative modifier), this is where your traveling gear comes into play! You may "spend" your traveling gear before or after the roll by erasing a check box to add +1 to your modifier. This represents how a nice sleep sack or the right treat can make all the difference!

You may share traveling gear between players.

Roll 1d6 on the Journey's End table and add this modifier to find out what toll the road has taken on you. Narrate why this is and how your character is feeling, then note any effects on your playbook.

All characters must do this individually.

> *Ordissa wraps up her narration. "We say goodbye to the treant and now it's time to see how we're doing after that one day of travel. Remember we just roll and then add +1 because we had 1 success and no failures during our journey."*
>
> *Maurine rolls a 1, adding +1 for a total of 2. The table says this will cost her -1 Morale, indicating the journey through the forest was a bit tiring. "Thankfully, I packed a special cooling cloth I like to bring around which makes the journey just a bit more comfortable and easy."*
>
> *This means she is going to spend one of her Gear to take +1 on the roll, bumping the 2 to a 3. The table says that the journey wasn't too bad; there is no effect, no loss of morale nor any gain.*

Arrival

Whether your journey was pleasant or harrowing, the best is yet to come! Your destination is near so take a moment to describe its location. Think on everything that's happened so far: the location of the inn itself; the terrain you've crossed; the descriptors you've noted.

What's going on?
What is this place like?

Then, at long last, you've arrived! You will then roll on a few more tables to discover more about your inn. If you're using a premade inn, there are descriptors ready for you to read. Otherwise, pick up those dice.

Type, Appearance, Etc.

Some of the tables are strictly aesthetical, meaning they have no bearing on the rules of the game. You may be tempted to gloss over these items but do not! Knowing that, say, the Screeching Pearl is in fact a thieves' den with stained glass windows will both help to cement the place in your imagination and give you material by which to narrate your revelries.

For, again, *The Broken Cask Society* relies on everyone to tell the tale of your journeys and having these descriptors to draw upon will make it that much more fun and easy.

Roll on the tables to discover the type of inn you're visiting, its appearance, and to meet any pets that may be malingering here.

Is this what you were expecting?
What do you think about it?

Finally, upon inspection, we can discover what level of Prestige this establishment has.

Prestige & Specialties

Prestige is a rough abstraction of the quality of the place you have reached. The sample inns in the reference chapter have set prestige levels, but if you are discovering an inn for the first time roll on the prestige table and take note.

The level of the inn affects your experience in some way, either because it's a wretched hive of scum and villainy, or because it's a regal establishment of uncomfortably stuffy repute. Also check your playbook because some characters will react to the prestige level, such as the pretentious Vintner.

Every inn and tavern, from the sloppiest alehouse to the most exquisite resort, has a specialty of the house. This will always prove to be interesting. Interesting could be good, like an exotic brew made from out-of-the-way gnomish spices, or it could be very bad. As the wise man once said "Here are the two words that should leap out at you when you navigate the menu: 'Monday' and 'Special'." Roll on the Specialties table and note it on your log.

If you are playing with a younger crowd, or wish to avoid alcohol, you may select this inn's specialty by hand to skip the booze.

While you will choose what courses you will partake of, you must always try the specialty of the house and you must always take disadvantage on this course the first time you try it. Why is that? Because sometimes specials are delicious but the expectation is so high that it affects your enjoyment. And sometimes the specials are really just experiments using yesterday's expired fish, making them even harder to enjoy.

Note the special and prepare your taste buds for adventure.

Arrival Event

Finally, as you step into the inn, check your bags, and take a look round, something is bound to happen.

Roll on the Arrival Event table to find out if (and what) happens when you go inside. This could be something as mundane as noting the cheerful atmosphere, or as awkward as seeing a rival Society member.

Results 2 and 3 will direct you to different tables. Simply follow the prompts and resolve as the events tell you to.

THE SOCIETY AWAITS

When playing with a group, you have the option of rolling one arrival event for the group or rolling one per player.

Ordissa was handed the dice and the tables. After a few rolls, she takes over as narrator again: "It seems the forest we just left has extended out to the town and inn itself. It's all natural looking with mossy walls and a roof made of purple vines. Inside on the right hand side is a fairly normal looking common room, even if the tables look like toadstools, but the left side is very weird and mystical."

"Like there's a row of druids just kind of meditating?" suggests Wulflen.

"Right, totally," says Ordissa.. "It's a prestige 4, so people know about this place far and wide…but it's fairly calm right now. Not a lot going on. Except…" She rolls on the Arrival Event table. "Carolton is here."

Maurine and Wulflen both laugh. Ordissa rolled a 3, which tells her that a Society rival is present and she needs to roll again on the Interference table. She rolls a 4, which says Carolton will behave himself and one of them will get a point of Mirth.

Ordissa plays the part of Carolton, taking on a sneering voice. "Oh hello, Maurine."

"Hello Carolton."

"I thought you'd make it here as well…but I wanted to check it out first. These types of lodges can be unsafe sometimes. Magic and all that. I wanted to scope it out first and make sure all was well."

Maurine says, in character, "Oh. Wow. Um, thank you Carolton. Want to join us for dinner?"

Ordissa, as Carolton, says, "No…thank you. I'm going to rest actually."

The table decides Maurine can have the point of Mirth.

Feasting

You're settled in now, ready to relax and enjoy the (hopefully) warm food and (again, hopefully) cold drink this place has on offer.

The feasting phase is a series of tests that tell us about the experience you have at the inn. You will choose your courses (including the special), then roll on a table to find out what exactly you're trying. You will test to see how you react to each course and, ultimately, how much fun you had feasting at the inn!

The Menu

The first step of feasting is figuring out what you'll be feasting on! As you saw when you rolled on the specialties table, there are six courses to any good dining experience:
- Beer
- Wine
- Soft Drinks
- Aperitif
- Entree
- Dessert

To create your menu, underline the specialty course on your society log, and then choose any combination of five other courses for a total of six. Tick these boxes on your log or write them down.

Again, once you have the special you can choose whatever you like. Five more food courses, all beer, all dessert, bit of coffee then a few entrees, whatever you like so long as the total is six and includes the specialty of the house.

> *Our trio settles in and looks over their options. They must choose a soft drink, as that is the special...and you know what? That sounds pretty good.*
>
> *"Let's just have three rounds of soft drinks!" cries Maurine.*
>
> *The rest shrug and agree. They'll move on to three entrees after the drink ceases to flow.*

Let's Eat!

Once the menu is set, take a moment to narrate:

> *What's going on?*
> *Where are you seated?*
> *Is it crowded or quiet?*

Then come the eats!

You can take your courses in any order. Do what you think they might do at this particular establishment. Then, find the appropriate course table and roll to discover what you're being served.

Just like any other test in this game, each food and drink item has a difficulty attached to it. This represents how challenging the item is in terms of its unfamiliar ingredients or preparation; in short, it's how hard it will be for your character to relax and enjoy this thing.

If you are playing with a group, decide ahead of time if you are all going to share each course or roll individually.

The random feasting tables do not have consequences. This is because each course is the same:
- Roll to find out what you're eating
- Narrate
- Test
- Narrate again
- On a hit, you mark Mirth because good food and drink makes you feel...well, mirthful!
- On a miss, you mark XP to show how your palate has expanded as you open yourself to new experiences, even if you don't like them. After that you roll on the React table.

If you are keeping score (see the Advanced Society Manual for more on that), be sure to mark on your log if each course was successful or not. Once this particular course is done, take some time to narrate then move on to the next.

Let's look at an example to make sure you know how this works.

> *The last few phases saw our trio to the Buzzing Elf Tavern (turns out the owner is particular about the name) and a rather uneventful arrival*

involving a discussion with Carolton. We rejoin them after they have chosen their menu, supped on a few soft drinks, and move along to the entree course.

"I'm ready for some food," says Wulflen. She flips to the Entree table and rolls d66. Her dice show 2 1, which the table says is Rack of Lamb with Mint Chutney. "Sounds heavy, but I'm sure it's good. The elvish server pops out from the kitchen carrying it and everybody watches it go by because it just smells so good. I grab my fork and knife and prepare to tuck in before they even set it down."

Maurine gestures toward Wulflen. "Can I snag some?"

"No!" Wulflen laughs. "Get your own."

"The server is still standing there," offers Ordissa.

"Oh, right," says Wulflen. "I tell him, 'It looks splendid. My compliments to the chef.' Now..."

She picks up a die and looks at her Gourmand playbook. "Well, I think I may have tasted this before," she says in reference ot the Gourmand move called Fond Memories. "And if I have then I can get +1 forward on this test...let's do that."

According to her move, she rolls 1d6 plus her Mind stat against an M3 test. She rolls a 1 and says, "Aw man...well, I can still mark XP. So I just can't quite remember where I've tasted something like this before...though it does seem familiar. I shake it off, take a big sniff, and cut a bite."

Wulflen rolls again to test against the B3 rack of lamb. She adds +1 for her Body stat, resulting in a 6!

"This lamb...is so good."

"I'm drooling," says Ordissa.

Because Wulflen hit this course, she marks a point of Mirth and notes that this course was a success.

THE REACT TABLE

Sometimes it's you, and sometimes it's the food. Except when it's the annoying bloke at the other table disturbing your meal. Or there's a kitchen fire. To find out what happens when a particular course just isn't vibing with you, roll on the react table.

A 1–3 means the food is just bad or you simply don't enjoy it. This may cost you morale, as journeying all this way for poor fare is simply demoralizing. Morale loss could also be physical — maybe that auroch's tongue is undercooked and offering you some tummy troubles! What's worse than a case of the scoots far from home?

Results 4 & 5 are extrinsic issues. That Society member who always gets on your nerves shows up at the wrong time or maybe a brawl breaks out. How uncouth!

A 6 means you grin and bear it and continue with the feast.

Unless otherwise stated by some other effect, like a playbook move or magical item, there is no modifier for the react table.

> *"'I'm going to have some!' And I reach across the table and snag a slice,"* says Ordissa, eager to try the delicious roast. She rolls, notes that her Body stat is a flat 0, and the die produces a miserly 1. She immediately clutches her stomach.
>
> *"Something's not tasting right,"* she says.
>
> Flipping to the React Table, Ordissa rolls again. The die shows a 2.
>
> *"Yeah, it's going down weird,"* she says. *"I think my tummy is rumbling."*
>
> The table tells her to roll again and to lose morale if she rolls a 1 or 2... thankfully it's a 4.
>
> *"I let out a massive belch,"* says Ordissa.
>
> *"Ew!"* shouts Maurine.
>
> Ordissa marks XP and suffers no other consequences. She says, *"Much better. Guess I won't try that again. What's next?"*
>
> *"You're nuts,"* laughs Wulflen.

Besides the food and drink itself, much else can happen during the feast phase. Make sure you're keeping track of conditions and taking note of who (or what!) is coming and going.

Sleep

It was a long journey and a (hopefully) enjoyable meal. Now it's time to settle in for a good night's sleep and a bit of digestion.

Unlike the react table there are several factors that modify your roll here. This includes the Prestige of the inn: a level 5 or 6 inn will give you +1 when you rest as the accommodations are so...accommodating. Several playbook moves such as the Campaigner, who always rests well, will influence the roll. There are also conditions along the way that can affect your rest. So, just like other rolls, consult your playbook and your notes before you roll on the sleep table.

Check your modifiers, roll on the table, and narrate accordingly.

> *It is Maurine's turn to narrate. "Well I'm stuffed. So I head upstairs to my room — I made sure we had separate rooms because Wulflen snores — change into my adorable pajamas and night cap and settle in with a sigh."*
>
> *Maurine flips to the sleep table and rolls without a modifier, as this inn is prestige level 4 and none of her moves or conditions affect the roll. She gets a 1.*
>
> *"What in the world?"*
>
> *The table tells her to find out what's going on at the inn, so she flips to the inn event table and rolls 2d6. The total of both dice is 8 which, according to the table, means some boisterous singing is going on!*
>
> *"Doesn't this town have a noise ordinance?" offers Ordissa.*
>
> *Maurine narrates. "With a sigh I hop out of bed and, still in my pink ogre pajamas, stomp downstairs. There's a goblin and two trolls singing about somebody's mother. Very rude. I shout, 'Hey! People are trying to sleep!'"*
>
> *Wulflen jumps in. "The innkeeper looks very anxious."*

"Well they should be!" says Maurine. The table says the difficulty of this test is H4, so she rolls. As a Vintner, her H is +1. The die shows a 2, +1 is 3. A miss!

"Wait a second, wait a second," she continues. "As you all know I'm very determined."

The rest nod in agreement. Maurine is referencing one of her traits, which will allow her to spend a point of Mirth to make the Expertise move.

"And I have that Mirth from earlier, so I'm going to spend it and use my expert determination to have another go," says Maurine.

She erases the tick mark on her book to spend the Mirth then rolls again. A 3 +1 for her Heart stat is a 4. She's hit the test!

"The carousers look ashamed," Maurine narrates. "I stamp my foot, looking very intimidating in my PJs, and they shuffle off. Now for a good sleep."

The sleep table says to ignore the usual inn event results and to instead take +1 Morale on a hit, so that's what she does.

Session End

Once you rest, it's time to decide: will you end the session or is there another inn to visit?

If the travels continue, return to the top of the Journey phase but skip the departure event. After that is is the same procedure: create the inn, make your journey, narrate, feast, have a good time.

If you are ending the session, there are a few things to do:
- Tidy up your playbook by erasing all advantages, complications, and conditions. The only things you get to keep are any items in your inventory and points of Mirth and XP. Morale and gear should remain unchanged.
- Choose to leave your story on a cliffhanger, or create an ending using the Epilogue table.
- Advance if you are using XP (see page 66)

And that's all there is to it! May your many journeys bring you many tasty treats and memorable stories and may the beer ever be cheap!

ADVANCED SOCIETY MANUAL

Well, initiate, it seems you've got a few journeys behind you and a sterling membership before you!

If you want to spice up (see what I did there?) your next session of *The Broken Cask Society* by adding a few tweaks to the rules or new dimension to the game world, read on.

Solitaire Options

The original Broken Cask is a solitaire game and so it is important that this game, while cooperative, be as friendly to solo gamers as possible. If you find your solitaire experience too challenging, or you just want to change it up, consider the following.

Elite Training

Without as many characters as in a multiplayer game, you are limited in the stats you may choose from to deal with particular events. If your character is weak in Wits, for example, you have no teammate to fill in that gap, even if you are able to spend Mirth. If you wish to avoid this difficulty, employ the Broken Cask Society's patented elite training regiment!

Cup of tea, ten squats, small beer, jog a mile, mugwort smoothie, repeat.

At the start of your first session, and your first session only, choose one stat and give it +1 just as if you'd advanced your character.

The Intern

Some solitaire gamers will opt to simply play as two characters. That is fine. If you want the stat boost without having to manage an entirely different character, however, the Broken Cask Society maintains a robust (and unpaid) internship programme.

Create your intern using the random character tables in the reference section and write it on either a notecard or the intern badge available in the playkit download. Any time you test, you may first roll 1d6 to represent the efforts of your intern to help you. If the roll shows a 4, 5, or 6 it is a hit and you may take +1 on that test.

Playing with a GM

Some groups will wish for a more traditional RPG experience and elect a player to become the Game Master. Play is exactly the same with a GM, but the players will never use random tables. Instead the GM will set the scene, the players will respond using their characters, and so on.

The GM may use their own stories, prompts, events, and challenges, or simply use the tables given to generate events and then elaborate upon them in setting the scene for the players.

We will not go further into how one plays as Game Master; there are many books out in the cosmos that can explain it more thoroughly. My own *Heavy Metal Thunder Mouse* has a robust chapter on GM'ing in general, as do many others; find a favorite if you need general help with the role. For now, here are some tips:

GM Tips

- Speak to the characters, not the players
- Always ask, "What happens next?"
- Nudge everything towards the cozy and tasty
- Narrate and present challenges with their playbooks in mind. This means that if you're playing with a stodgy Vintner, for example, they should be presented with yucky, uncomfortable situations where they feel out of place and not a comfortable trip to a winery they know (unless that's the type of game you're running)
- Consider what's going on in the world away from the current scene at all times

- Only test when the outcome is uncertain and failure can be interesting
- Have a few NPCs created and written down so you can introduce them to the story as needed
- Always say "Yes!" unless you have a very good reason not to

Society Standings

Those players with a competitive spirit may wish to incorporate standings into their games. This is a list of the five most winsome Broken Cask Society members on prominent display in the main salon/parlour of the Society house.

It should be created while you prepare to play and then updated at the end of each session by using the following rules:

Create the Board

Before the first session, create the board by generating a total of five Society members already on the board. These characters may fall off the board as you and your friends overtake them, but begin with five. Use the tables in the reference section starting on page 87 (or the character tables in the original Broken Cask). Write them down on a piece of paper or print out the Society Standings Board on page 83.

Once character are created and written down, use the table on the next page to find out each characters starting score.

There! The standings board is created.

Tally Score

As you play *The Broken Cask Society*, players should track their scores as they go. The score for Broken Cask Society Standings is calculated as follows:

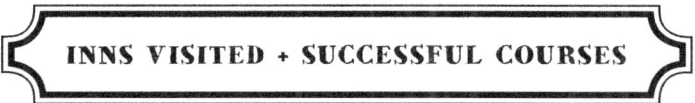

INNS VISITED + SUCCESSFUL COURSES

To clarify, a successful course is any food or drink test you hit during the Feast phase of play and should be marked with a check on your log.

Update the Board

When you end your session, update the board by totaling up the player scores, then randomly modify the existing member scores using this table.

2d6	SCORE MODIFIER
2	-4
3	-3
4	-2
5	-1
6	0
7	+1
8	+2
9	+3
10	+4
11	+5
12	+6

Improvement

Broken Cask Society is designed with the one shot in mind, one fun night of stamping around the world on a kind of fantastical pub crawl. However there are options in place for campaigns that could span many sessions. One optional rule some will want to include is that of improvement.

Improving your character is just another way of saying "level up." When you fill your character's XP bar you may, **at the end of the session**, choose one of the following options to improve your character:
- Check a new move
- Check or write a new Personality trait
- Add another permanent box of Morale
- Add another permanent box of Gear
- Add 1 to any stat (Body, Mind, or Heart) to a maximum of +3

When adding a new trait, it cannot be a background trait. This is a piece of your history that is fixed and so not discoverable unless you want to deal with some kind of amnesiac plot device. So when you add a new trait, it must be a new Personality trait. This can be one of the pre-written traits or there is space to create your own.

Go back to character creation on page 27 to read up on writing your own traits.

Rapid Advancement

Normally, once your XP bar is full it's full: you cannot add more until the end of the session, after you spend that XP to improve and then erase your fancy checkmarks.

However if you want to advance more quickly you can continue to add XP whenever it happens beyond the limitations of those boxes. Simple tally the extra points on your playbook or draw in some more XP boxes.

Advancing quickly means you can explore your character options more rapidly and grow in prowess from session to session at a rate exceeding that of mere mortal Society expeditioners. This can be fun for players wishing to try out different moves and build or who just want to make the game a tad easier.

Have you got your own hacks and house rule? I want to hear about it! Find me online @ShorelessSkies!

The Finest Inns

Throughout the relatively brief history of our Society, some locales have already fallen into the realm of legends. These are a few of them. The rest are kept in the Great Ledger. The following is a selection of three of the best-known inns throughout the land. If your travels take you there, be sure to stop by and tell them Korm sent you.

Use these inns during your games if you wish. If you do so, you can skip inn generation and many journey rolls. Be sure to include the specialty in your menu!

You can find many more inns, and add your own, at the Great Ledger on ShorelessSkies.com!

The Bright Casket

Proprietor: Grimm the Grim
Staff: Nokturno (Human? Barkeep); Abbaf (Half-ork Vegan Chef); Nefaz (Human Sommelier/Undertaker)
Prestige: 3
Type: Tavern/Mortuary
Specialty: Corpse Reviver (Soft Drinks)
Appearance: Dark, mysterious, otherworldly
Pets: A trio of singing rats
Terrain: Riverlands
Days of Travel: 2
Settlement Type: A dusty old town

Settled atop a pile of bones in the middle of town, the Bright Casket has served its patrons (live and undead) for generations with a toothsome grin and a dirty mug. Most come for the dark and moody atmosphere; others come to try the specialty drinks and fine crudité.

It's said that this place was little more than a dive before Boniface jump-started the affair, then the morbid innkeeper took his haunted aesthetic and ran with it. This is the result.

The Egret & Infant

Proprietor: Gastin, goblin profiteer
Staff: Lilypush (Satyr Porter); Taklimashan (Human Concierge); Marsden (Elf Line Cook)
Prestige: 6
Type: Post Stop
Specialty: Lofty Pint (Ale)
Appearance: Elegant, polished wood and fine velvet carpets
Pets: Primo the Poodle
Terrain: Mountains
Days of Travel: 2
Settlement Type: A charming village

It's a bit of a climb, but snug inside the alpine of Burgle Mountain is a cave that's not a cave. Once inside, the Egret & Infant has all the comforts of a spa or resort, just at a certain altitude. Their primary patrons are lindworm pilots, who rest their serpentine mounts and sip hardy beer until their next deliveries are due. Non-pilots are welcome as well, though it takes a bit of doing to get up there. All admit it is worth the trip.

The Green Crow Inn

Proprietor: Kalka of the Gindi
Staff: Furrier (Troll Cellarer); Sumi Kind (Dwarf Barback)
Prestige: 4
Type: Country Inn
Specialty: Dandelion Tart (Dessert)
Appearance: Rustic and pleasant
Pets: None (ask Furrier)
Terrain: Plains
Days of Travel: 3
Settlement Type: A charming hamlet called Niwari

Innkeeper Kalka will never confirm it, but the story goes that the Green Crow once belonged to her grandmother. Her parents, impetuous and broke, sold the inn for a tidy sum. When Kalka came of age she bought it back and has worked to make it the finest establishment it can be. On the outskirts of a small town, it rests as a pleasant and welcoming spot for comers of all kinds and ages looking for a comfortable nights rest and a tasty sup for the road.

REFERENCE

Here lies the meat and potatoes of the game: random tables to use during play, playbooks to peruse, society logs to mark, and so on.

Before we say goodbye, thanks for checking out *The Broken Cask Society*! Questions? Find me at ShorelessSkies.com and everywhere else @ShorelessSkies.

RULES CLARIFICATION

What about money? Why do I have no gold?
All your expenses are covered by your Society dues, so you need not track your expenses.

What's with some of these names?
Does this fantasy world really have a Chianti region?
Shhhhhhhh...

We have to add a day to the journey but it doesn't say who it affects.
Journeys always include all characters.

I got a mount and I want to use it to skip a day.
What about my friends?
You leave them in the dust! If, for example, you have 2 days left and you use your mount to skip one, they roll for their next Adventure without you then you test the final adventure as a group again.

What does 10 on the Riverland table mean?
If you miss you have the option of marking the day as a failure, or treating is as a success but adding another day to the journey. Cost-benefit, baby!

What's the deal with the Gourmand's "Common Cause" move?
Basically you make an NPC a friend and then they can help you with something. The table has to agree that the effect is reasonable. If you're playing solo, it's between you and your conscience. Examples include +1 forward, canceling a test, taking advantage on a table, things like that.

Who gets to act again?
While playing with a group, all players may act on an event, even if the book does not say so. But all acting players suffer Hits and Misses individually.

REFERENCE

The stat being tested doesn't seem to match the event. What gives?
Whenever possible, the stat is meant to go along with the event in question (so, a test involving other characters would most often use the Heart stat). However mechanical balance is paramount, so all stats had to be represented as equally as possible. If a stat doesn't seem to properly match to its test, take it as an opportunity to narrate in creative ways.

I have advantage forward and disadvantage forward. What do I do?
In this case it's up to player discretion. You can choose to allow them to cancel each other out, or resolve one this roll then the other on the next roll.

Can't I just spend Mirth to succeed during the Feast, wwthen get the Mirth back?
Mirth is not always a guarantee of success, but yes. This is a viable strategy. You may also want to risk failure just for the XP!

I have disadvantage forward because of the Prestige level of the inn and because of my playbook. How does that work?
You take disadvantage for your next two rolls!

PLAYBOOKS

*The playbooks here are presented in brief.
The full sheets are available in the play materials.*

THE CAMPAIGNER

You are a hardy sort, used to the difficulties of a soldierly life.

Background Traits: ■ Veteran ■ Mercenary ■ Royal Guard

Stats: Body +2 | Mind -1 | Heart

Campaigner Moves:
- ■ Rough & Ready – Add 1 permanent Morale box to your playbook

- ■ Iron Gut – when you would roll on the **React** table, make a B4 Test. On a hit you can choose what happens. On a miss take +1 when you roll on that table.

- ■ Unending Stamina – When you would become **Exhausted**, make a B3 test. On a hit you do not become Exhausted and heal +1 Morale; on a miss you may choose which stat becomes exhausted, even if the table says otherwise.

- ✓ Quick Tempered – whenever someone **Interferes** take -1 forward (after you roll on the Interference table).

The Vintner

You have the manners of a maid and the palate of a low-level god.

Background Traits: ■Restaurateur ■Former Adventurer ■Enthusiastic Amateur

Stats: Body -1 | Mind +1 | Heart +1

Vintner Moves

- ■ The Nose Knows – When you would test and your sense of smell can help, make a M4 test. On a hit you succeed automatically; on a miss take +1 on that test.

- ■ Exquisite Taste – Take advantage forward at any inn with Prestige 3-6; take disadvantage forward at an inn of Prestige 1-2

- ■ Wine Talk – On any event involving other characters, make a H3 test. You may spend XP (erase a ✓) to boost this roll. On a hit you may avoid having to test or take +1 Mirth; on a miss mark XP and then test as usual.

- ✓ Hyper Analytical – "Is this a bordeaux? No…it must be Anorian… no…" Whenever you test involving wine take +1 forward; if you miss any test involving wine, take disadvantage when you next roll on the Rest table.

The Pilgrim

You are a traveler of great experience.

Background Traits: ■ Religious ■ Adventure seeker ■Shepherd

Stats: Body 0 | Mind 0 | Heart +1

Pilgrim Moves

- ■ Well-traveled – Circle 1 type: Plains | Mountains | Forest | Desert | Riverlands | Tundra

- ■ Before you roll on the Adventure table for this type, make a H4 test. On a hit you know the way and may choose the event yourself; on a miss take +1 forward.

- Friend to Beasts – Before any test involving animals make a H3 test. On a hit, skip the test as if you succeeded and explain what the animal has told you; on a miss, take +1 forward.

- Leave None to Waste – Any time an event tells you to take +1 Morale, Gear, or Mirth, but you cannot restore either, check a circle here. When you would lose any on a later event, spend this first:
  ○ Extra Morale ○ Extra Gear ○ Extra Mirth

- ✓ Out of Doors – You are too used to sleeping on the ground. Take -1 any time you Rest at a Prestige 4-6 inn.

The Kegmaster

You are a brewer of great skill and curiosity.

Background Traits: ■ Homebrewer ■ Alchemist ■ Retired Chef

Stats: Body +1 | Mind +1 | Heart -1

Kegmaster Moves:

- Drunk Luck – Once during a Journey, make a M3 test. On a hit you may choose the next Adventure instead of rolling on the table; on a miss you may flip the next test result on this Adventure.

- Potions – Pass a M2 test to remove the Exhausted condition from anyone; on a miss you take -1 Morale.

- Beer Diplomacy – Add another Gear box. Besides Journey's End, you may spend Gear to take +1 on any test involving other characters.

- ✓ Kegmaster – You are hard to impress. You must always try the ale when you feast and whenever you test for that course take -1.

The Gourmand

Your life is a perpetual hunt for new flavors.

Background Traits: ■Restaurateur ■Academic ■Retired Chef

Stats: Body +1 | Mind +1 | Heart -1

Gourmand Moves
- Fond Memories – If you think you've tasted this before, make a M3 test. On a hit take +1 Mirth; on a miss mark XP.

- Palatial Palate – You never take disadvantage on the special.

- Common Cause – When you are at an inn you can always find someone to talk to about food. If you want their help, make a H3 test. On a hit they can help you within reason; on a miss you offend them and take disadvantage forward.

- Cookbook Research – You are working on an amazing cookbook. Whenever you hit on a test involving food, make a M3 test. On a hit, mark XP; on a miss nothing happens.

- ✓ Reputation – If you ever encounter a Society rival at a Prestige 1-3 inn, take disadvantage forward.

LOG

Session Date

Characters & Players

NPCs

Other Notes

Journey the First

No. of Days ~~~~~~~~~~~~~~~~~~~~~~~~~~~~~~~~

Inn Name ~~~~~~~~~~~~~~~~~~~~~~~~~~~~~~~~

~~~~~~~~~~~~~~~~~~~~~~~~~~~~~~~~

Landscape

- ■ Plains   ■ Mountains   ■ Forest
- ■ Desert   ■ Riverlands   ■ Tundra

Adventures
Note hits with ✓ and misses with ✗

■ ■ ■ ■ ■ ■

Prestige

■ 1   ■ 2   ■ 3   ■ 4   ■ 5   ■ 6

Feast!
✓ the Special (Disadvantage on that table) and underline the other courses to total 3 beverage & 3 food

- ■ Ale   ■ Wine   ■ Soft Drinks
- ■ Entree   ■ Aperitif   ■ Desserts

Favorite Course ~~~~~~~~~~~~~~~~~~~~~~~~~~~~~~~~

Events & Notes

~~~~~~~~~~~~~~~~~~~~~~~~~~~~~~~~

~~~~~~~~~~~~~~~~~~~~~~~~~~~~~~~~

~~~~~~~~~~~~~~~~~~~~~~~~~~~~~~~~

~~~~~~~~~~~~~~~~~~~~~~~~~~~~~~~~

~~~~~~~~~~~~~~~~~~~~~~~~~~~~~~~~

~~~~~~~~~~~~~~~~~~~~~~~~~~~~~~~~

~~~~~~~~~~~~~~~~~~~~~~~~~~~~~~~~

Journey the Second

REFERENCE

No. of Days ⟨⟨⟨⟨⟩⟩⟩⟩

Inn Name ⟨⟨⟨⟨⟩⟩⟩⟩

⟨⟨⟨⟨⟩⟩⟩⟩

Landscape
- ☐ Plains ☐ Mountains ☐ Forest
- ☐ Desert ☐ Riverlands ☐ Tundra

Adventures
Note hits with ✓ and misses with ✗
☐ ☐ ☐ ☐ ☐ ☐

Prestige
☐ 1 ☐ 2 ☐ 3 ☐ 4 ☐ 5 ☐ 6

Feast!
✓ the Special (Disadvantage on that table) and underline the other courses to total 3 beverage & 3 food

- ☐ Ale ☐ Wine ☐ Soft Drinks
- ☐ Entree ☐ Aperitif ☐ Desserts

Favorite Course ⟨⟨⟨⟨⟩⟩⟩⟩

Events & Notes

⟨⟨⟨⟨⟩⟩⟩⟩

⟨⟨⟨⟨⟩⟩⟩⟩

⟨⟨⟨⟨⟩⟩⟩⟩

⟨⟨⟨⟨⟩⟩⟩⟩

⟨⟨⟨⟨⟩⟩⟩⟩

⟨⟨⟨⟨⟩⟩⟩⟩

⟨⟨⟨⟨⟩⟩⟩⟩

Journey the Third

No. of Days ⁓⁓⁓⁓⁓⁓⁓⁓⁓⁓⁓⁓⁓⁓⁓⁓⁓⁓⁓⁓⁓⁓⁓⁓⁓⁓⁓⁓

Inn Name ⁓⁓⁓⁓⁓⁓⁓⁓⁓⁓⁓⁓⁓⁓⁓⁓⁓⁓⁓⁓⁓⁓⁓⁓⁓⁓⁓⁓

⁓⁓⁓⁓⁓⁓⁓⁓⁓⁓⁓⁓⁓⁓⁓⁓⁓⁓⁓⁓⁓⁓⁓⁓⁓⁓⁓⁓

Landscape
- ■ Plains
- ■ Mountains
- ■ Forest
- ■ Desert
- ■ Riverlands
- ■ Tundra

Adventures
Note hits with ✓ and misses with ✗

■ ■ ■ ■ ■ ■

Prestige
■ 1   ■ 2   ■ 3   ■ 4   ■ 5   ■ 6

Feast!
*✓ the Special (Disadvantage on that table) and
underline the other courses to total 3 beverage & 3 food*

- ■ Ale
- ■ Wine
- ■ Soft Drinks
- ■ Entree
- ■ Aperitif
- ■ Desserts

Favorite Course ⁓⁓⁓⁓⁓⁓⁓⁓⁓⁓⁓⁓⁓⁓⁓⁓⁓⁓⁓⁓⁓⁓⁓⁓⁓⁓⁓⁓⁓⁓⁓⁓⁓⁓⁓⁓⁓

Events & Notes

STANDINGS BOARD

1d6	MEMBER NAME	DESCRIPTION	CURRENT SCORE

SESSION OUTLINE

★ Prepare
in which we make ready for what lies ahead

- Prepare your playbook
  - If this is the first session, check all Morale & Gear boxes
- Introduce characters individually:
  Who are you?
  Why are you a part of this Society?
  How are you getting ready to leave?
- Each player may choose 1 Preparation from the table and narrate

★ Journey
- **Set Out** – in which we gather at the Society House
  - Each player may roll on the Departure Event table
  - You meet up at the Broken Cask Society House:
    How do you all know each other?
    Is there a reason you are traveling together?
    Why are you traveling alone?
    What is the Society House like?
  - Roll to find out the Inn location & Name
    How did you hear about this inn?
  - Use the tables to find out more about your journey:
    ◇ Roll for Terrain and Travel Time –
    each day brings 1 Adventure (see below)
  - Now describe your first day on the road:
    What are you doing?
    What is the weather like?
- **Adventure** – in which the road brings us something unexpected
  - Use tables and roll to determine time of day and the specific event:
    What's happened?
  - Decide who is going to act and then test to resolve:
    What did you do and what happens next?
  - Mark Adventure as successful ✓ or unsuccessful ✗ on the Log

- If there are more days left to journey, have another Adventure, otherwise proceed
- **Journey's End** – in which we see what toll the journey has taken
    - Create modifier by totaling your Adventure results: +1 for ✓ and -1 for ✗
        - Can spend Gear for +1 on this roll individually
    - Each player rolls on the Journey's End table, applying their modifier.
    What happened?
    How are you feeling?
    - Erase any temporary effects you may have gained from the Journey

★ Arrive
in which our journey ends and we gain a first impression of the inn

What is the location like? What is going on?

- Roll to discover more about the inn: its type, its appearance, its Prestige level, specialties of the house, and any pets that may live there, and take note of these.
Is this what you were expecting? What do you think about it?

- Roll Arrival Event.
What happens next?

★ Feast
in which we eat, drink, and judge

- Take a seat and create your menu by choosing any combination of 3 beverage courses (must include the special)
    - Ale
    - Wine
    - Soft Drink
- And any combination of 3 food courses (must include the special)
    - Aperitif
    - Entree
    - Dessert

For example, a menu could have 2 Ales, 1 Wine, and 3 aperitifs if the Wine is the specialty.

- For every course, each player will test to see how their characters react, and then narrate accordingly
  - Roll d66 on the appropriate table and test
  - Take +1 Mirth on a hit as you were able to appreciate the flavor profile of this course
  - On a miss mark XP and then roll on the React table.

★ Rest
in which we retire and digest

How was your meal?
What else happened at the inn?

- Check for any modifiers
- Roll on the Rest table
  How do you feel at the end of your visit?
- Refresh playbook by erasing any Exhaustion, Sickness, etc.
- Begin the next journey (skipping the Prepare phase) or end the session

★ Session End
- Narrate our epilogue or roll for it on the epilogue table
- Tidy notes by clearing all advantages, complications, and conditions (keep items, Mirth, and XP)
- Improve (optional) – if you have filled your XP bar you may choose one:
  - Add another Morale box
  - Add another Gear box
  - Select a new Move
  - Select a new Personality Trait
  - +1 to any stat (max +3)

REFERENCE

TABLES

Use the tables on the following pages to inspire the beats of your story. The tables tell you what dice to roll — 1d6, 2d6, or d66 — and provide a range of prompts. After your prompt is determined, it is up to you to describe what happens next and how your character reacts. Roll again to see how your character does and follow what the table says if you hit or miss.

Optional tables are indicated with a star (*) in the header. These tables are here to help you further flesh out your stories and generate plot action, but they are not necessary.

Two stars (**) means, if you are playing in a group, you may either roll once for the entire group, or, unless otherwise noted, all players may roll individually.

The tables are also available as a PDF that can be viewed on a laptop or tablet, or printed out. Additionally, the tables can be accessed using the Broken Cask Society app.

All of these resources can be found at ShorelessSkies.com or by scanning this QR code . . .

Prepare

Choose one from this table.

PREPARATION TABLE*
Shop by rolling on the market table
Pack and add +1 Gear box to your playbook for this Journey only
Make merry for 1 point of Mirth
Relax and take +1 Morale (even above your max amount)

Inn creation

When you Set Out, start by rolling to find the location of the next inn and its name. You might use the inn names from the original Broken Cask if you like.

2d6	THE NEXT INN IS LOCATED...	2d6	THIS PART of the WORLD IS...*
2	Atop a sleeping creature	2	Tense
3	Among the treetops	3	Peaceful
4	In the middle of nowhere	4	Boorish
5	Near a spiritual center	5	Historic
6	In or near a desert	6	Mundane
7	The center of town	7	Bustling
8	At the edge of a big city	8	Cosmopolitan
9	Underground	9	Wealthy
10	Over a river	10	Quiet
11	Near a magical place	11	Destitute
12	Between planes of existence	12	Volatile

d66	INN NAME	d66	INN NAME
11	Thieving	11	Hand
12	Wondering	12	Goblin
13	Conniving	13	Plough
14	Singing	14	Maid
15	Playing	15	Child
16	Barking	16	Stag
21	Sitting	21	Diamond
22	Watching	22	Crown
23	Learning	23	Toadstool
24	Cutting	24	Cauldron
25	Dancing	25	Dwarf
26	Smoking	26	Monk
31	Sojourning	31	Kobold
32	Shaving	32	Mitre
33	Writing	33	Gargoyle
34	Resting	34	Dirk
35	Buzzing	35	Mountain
36	Herding	36	Rosebud
41	Flowering	41	Helm
42	Farming	42	Elf
43	Warring	43	Marigold
44	Keeping	44	Porridge
45	Caring	45	Porter
46	Reigning	46	Fir
51	Shaking	51	Twig
52	Scratching	52	Duck
53	Racing	53	Lampost
54	Reaching	54	Stitch
55	Guarding	55	Kraken
56	Threading	56	Wolf
61	Gleaning	61	Star
62	Beholding	62	Armsman
63	Glimmering	63	Forge
64	Fruiting	64	Foxglove
65	Leeching	65	Daisy
66	Professing	66	Briar

Depart

When you leave, something may happen.

1d6	DEPARTURE EVENT*
1	A loved one offers their blessing. Who are they? Take a point of Mirth.
2	A Society rival has left you a nasty note. What does it say? Take -1H forward.
3	You found an extra bit of tack from your last journey! +1 when you roll on the Journey's End table
4	Reports of nasty weather come your way. What's going on? Take disadvantage when you roll on an Adventure table.
5	A retiring Society members offers you their rusty old weapon. Who are they? You can spend this weapon to take +1 on any appropriate test.
6	You discover you have time for breakfast. Roll on the Breakfast table.

1d6	BREAKFAST	EFFECT
1	Coffee	Just the thing to get the Journey started. Take advantage when you roll on the journey length table.
2	Tea	Refreshing. Take +1 Adventure forward.
3	Bread	Perfectly sustaining! +1 Mirth
4	Pastry	Choose: Eat it now for +1 Morale or spend it later to take advantage when you roll on the Arrival Event table.
5	Eggs	These aren't sitting right for some reason. Take note.
6	Porridge	Filling and satisfying. Take advantage forward.

Journey

How many days and what terrain?

1d6	DAYS of TRAVEL One Adventure per Day
1	4 days of travel
2	3 days of travel
3	3 days of travel
4	2 days of travel
5	2 day of travel
6	1 day of travel

You must traverse across...

1d6	DESCRIPTOR*	1d6	TYPE
1	Barren	1	Plains
2	Wild	2	Mountain
3	Lively	3	Riverlands
4	Magical	4	Forest
5	Dense	5	Desert
6	Pleasant	6	Tundra

Adventure

Roll to see when the event is taking place during your day, then roll on the appropriate table to find out what happens next and then resolve the event.

1d6	TIME OF EVENT*
1	Dawn
2	Late Morning
3	Midday
4	Afternoon
5	Dusk
6	Midnight

PLAINS**

2d6	EVENT	HIT	MISS
2	M3: A dense fog rolls in. How do you navigate it?	Acting character(s) take +1H forward for this journey.	-1 Journey forward
3	B3: Something has gotten into the rations. What happens next?	You manage to salvage a few morsels and make a feast of it! +1 Mirth	You must dig into the spare rations. All characters -1 Gear
4	H3: A caravan passes by. How will you get their attention?	You manage to stop the caravan and discover they have wares for sale! You may roll on the Market table.	This caravan is... long. Mark XP then roll. On a 1 or 2 you must wait. +1 Day to your Journey.
5	B4: The firewood has gotten wet. How will you get it going?	You get the fire going anyway and rest well. All characters take +1 forward.	A cold and miserable night costs all characters -1 Morale
6	H4: Where is that one thing?!	Oh, it was here the whole time.	Acting character(s) choose 1 item to remove, or suffers -1M forward.

REFERENCE

2d6	EVENT	HIT	MISS
7	M4: You come upon a patch of wild vegetables. How do you approach them?	You pick the right ones. All characters choose: +1 Gear or +1 Morale.	Not that one! Acting character(s) marks XP and becomes Sick
8	H5: Sounds along the road rattle your nerves. What do you do? All characters test.	You manage to find quiet and rest well at the end of the day. +1 Mirth	The noises are inescapable and ruin your sleep.
9	B5 Wild animals are crossing the road. Roll on the fauna table. How do you avoid their attention?	They pass more swiftly than you expected and you continue on your journey.	The alpha attacks! Acting character(s) suffers -1d3 Morale and marks XP
10	M6: Unending plains shake your spirit. How do you cope? All characters test.	The distance isn't so bad.	The distance is daunting. All characters mark XP and take -1H forward
11	H7: A thunderstorm swiftly rolls in. Where do you look for shelter?	You find shelter. Acting character(s) takes +1 Mirth or +1 Morale after a night of song.	You are soaked and unable to sleep. All characters -1 Morale
12	B6: Use your tools and wits to orientate.	Subtract 1 day from your journey	You are lost. +1 day to this Journey.

MOUNTAIN**

2d6	EVENT	HIT	MISS
2	M3: Where is that one thing?!	Oh, it was here the whole time.	Acting character(s) chooses 1 item to remove, or suffers -1M forward.
3	B3: Terrible weather rolls in off the top of the mountains. What do you do?	You negotiate the storm skillfully and with a story to tell. Acting character(s) takes +1 Mirth	You are kept awake all night trying to survive the storm. Acting character(s) mars XP.
4	H3 The chill of freezing mountain winds cuts through your clothes. What do you do?	After a night spent huddling for warmth, you emerge with great resolution. Acting character(s) takes +1 Mirth	You get no rest, for you must keep moving to stay warm. All characters -1 Morale
5	B4: Steep cliffs stand before you. How do you approach them?	One of the footholds is actually the den of a tiny, helpful sprite. Roll. On a 1-2 they offer to become the acting character(s) familiar (see the rare items table below).	You are able to climb up but at a hefty physical toll. Acting character(s) takes disadvantage when you roll on the Journey's End table.
6	H4: In a valley you come upon a stream to ford. What do you do?	Crossing is easier than expected!	It's extremely slippery. All characters mark XP and roll. On a 1-2 become Exhausted in body.

2d6	EVENT	HIT	MISS
7	M4: Growing off the side of the mountain are some wild mushrooms. What do you do?	After carefully evaluation, you are able to pack some away. Acting character(s) chooses: +1 Gear or +1 Morale.	These are definitely not safe to eat. Acting character(s) should roll. On a 1-2 become Sick.
8	H5: A peaceful glade opens up. What do you do to investigate it?	You are able to find a place to rest briefly. All characters take +1 when you roll on the Journey's End table.	You stumble upon a thicket of brambles and waste a few hours getting through.
9	B5 Mountain Goat Strike! How do you defend yourself?	You are able to safely shoo away the fell beast.	The beast pounces upon you with hate. Acting character(s) marks XP and take -1 Morale.
10	M6: The mountains rumble. Snow and rocks begin to slide. What do you do?	You clear away quick enough and the slide actually makes a way for you. Acting character(s) takes +1B Forward	It's going to take an extra day to get around this. +1 day to this Journey
11	H7: Some giants are having a thunder battle! What do you do?	Those giants are actually quite helpful and show you a shortcut. All characters take advantage when you roll on the Journey's End table.	Rocks everywhere! Acting character(s) is struck on the head and should take note.
12	B6: Orientate	Subtract 1 day from your journey	You are lost. +1 day to this Journey.

RIVERLAND**

2d6	EVENT	HIT	MISS
2	M3: Where is that one thing?!	Oh, it was here the whole time.	Acting character(s) chooses 1 item to remove, or suffers -1M forward.
3	B3: Cramps! How will you ease them out?	You are able to work through the pain and feel a certain confidence. Acting character(s) takes +1B forward.	It hurts so bad! Acting character(s) marks XP and becomes Poisoned.
4	H3 Rain clouds threaten. What do you do?	You find shelter in time for a restful night sleep.	You cannot find safety and spend a miserable night in the rain.
5	B4: Fish splash in a nearby pool. How will you get them?	You are able to catch a few! All characters choose: +1 Morale or +1 Mirth	The fish drag you into the water. Acting character(s) takes -1 Morale
6	H4 A bog wight appears and is eager to chat. How will you handle the conversation?	You are able to catch them up on the recent news from outside and they offer a shortcut. Spend 1 gear to take -1 day from this Journey	You cannot breakaway from the conversation and it's so boring. +1 day to this Journey

REFERENCE

2d6	EVENT	HIT	MISS
7	M4: You come across a patch of river flowers. How do you investigate?	With care they can be used to heal! All characters choose +1 Morale or +1 Mirth	A spray of pollen starts you coughing. Acting character(s) marks XP and becomes poisoned.
8	H5: The shadow of dark things flying overhead is...unsettling. How do you cope? All characters test	You forge ahead with determination. All characters +1H forward.	The threat of whatever-it-is is too much right now. All characters take disadvantage forward.
9	B5 The riverbanks are flooded. How will you cross?	You are able to find a path and carry on.	It's too mucky to pass. +1 day to this Journey
10	M6 The river branches in a few different directions. Which way will you go?	You path takes you to a makeshift camp of traders. All characters may roll on the Market table.	The water is perilous here and you must backtrack. Choose: treat this test as a hit but take +1 day on this Journey or take the miss and continue.
11	H7: A pack of bandits guard the river crossing. How do you deal with them?	You manage to run them off with some ease! Acting character(s) chooses: +1 Mirth or Advantage forward	They get in a few hits before you defeat them. All characters mark XP and suffer -1 Morale.
12	B6: Orientate	Subtract 1 day from your journey	You are lost. +1 day to this Journey.

FOREST**

2d6	EVENT	HIT	MISS
2	M3: Where is that one thing?!	Oh, it was here the whole time.	Acting character(s) chooses 1 item to remove, or suffers -1M forward.
3	B3 There is a dense thicket before you. How do you approach it?	You press through with little delay.	All of your things become snagged and some items are lost. All characters -1 Gear
4	H3 The sounds of the forest are oppressive. How will you keep calm?	You muster your courage and continue on. All characters take +1H forward	It's a bit much. All characters disadvantage forward.
5	B4: Small game appear. Lunch?	Lunch! All characters choose: +1 Morale or +1 Mirth	They escape your grasp to great frustration. Acting character(s) -1H forward
6	H4 A Giant Treant emerges, looking for friends. What do you say?	They offer to show you a shortcut. Any character *may* spend 1 Gear to move to Journey's End now.	Whatever you've said has made them angry and they chase you off. +1 Day to this Journey

REFERENCE

2d6	EVENT	HIT	MISS
7	M4: A windstorm is picking up. What do you do?	You find shelter with time enough for a lovely lunch.	All characters -1 XP or -1H forward
8	H5 Spider webs block your path. How do you get through?	You hear the spiders cursing their bad luck behind you. +1 B forward.	You barely break free before the spiders make a snack of you. No rest will be found tonight.
9	M5 You find a patch of wild fruit. How do you harvest it?	After carefully evaluation, you are able to pack some away. All characters choose: +1 Gear or +1 Morale	These are definitely not safe to eat. Acting character(s) marks XP and rolls. On a 1-2 become Sick.
10	B6: A tree limb snaps overhead. All characters must test.	You dive out of the way in time! Choose: assist a comrade who has missed their roll or +1 Mirth.	That hurts. Mark XP and suffer -1 Morale
11	Flip H7 A shaman of the Frogfolk halts you! How do you approach them?	They're actually quite nice and offer you a good resting spot. Acting character(s) takes +1 when they roll on the Journey's End table	What? What tastes like purple? All characters become ensorceled.
12	B5: Orientate	Subtract 1 day from your journey	You are lost. +1 day to this Journey.

DESERT**

2d6	EVENT	HIT	MISS
2	M3: Where is that one thing?!	Oh, it was here the whole time.	Acting character(s) chooses 1 item to remove, or suffers -1M forward.
3	B3: The heat beats you down. How will you go on? All characters test.	We must advance! For the Society! Take +1H forward	You must spend some of your reserves to quench your parched palate. -1 Gear
4	H3 Sounds emanate from a small cave. How do you approach? Test M3. On a hit you are sneaky enough to take advantage on this test.	You get the drop on what appear to be a small pack of gnomish wanderers. They teach you a merry tune. Acting character(s) takes Advantage forward.	Whoever it was has scarpered, leaving you bored and unfulfilled.
5	Flip B4: A few small animals scurry across the sands. Lunch?	Lunch! All characters choose: +1 Morale or +1 Gear	They escape your grasp to great frustration. Acting character(s) -1H forward
6	H4 You think you spy a Society rival stumbling across the dunes. Who are they? How do you help?	They are grateful and offer to spread word of your kindness through the Society. All characters take +1 Mirth.	You make some misstep. What is it? They complain incessantly, causing all characters -1H forward. Acting character(s) marks XP.

REFERENCE

2d6	EVENT	HIT	MISS
7	M4: A patch of cacti is here near a small oasis. How do you harvest it?	Fresh water! Acting character(s) chooses: +1 Gear or +1 Morale	Just a mirage. Acting character(s) marks XP and suffer -1 Morale
8	H5: A massive black obelisk stands tall in the middle of the desert. How do you approach it?	It vibrates in knowing fashion and you feel the secrets of the universe are within reach. Acting character(s) takes note.	Bad! Definitely bad! It feels like a bad dream. Acting character(s) becomes Ensorceled.
9	B5 Desert Imps harass you. How do you fend them off?	Whatever you did worked and they offer you a gift. Acting character(s) may roll on the Market table.	You manage to fight them off but it is hard work. All characters roll. On a 1-2 become Exhausted in Body.
10	Flip M6: A sandstorm is visible on the horizon. How do you find shelter?	You stumble into a cave with a water supply. All characters choose +1 Gear or +1 Morale	The storm pushes you into a mysterious cave full of swirling spirits. You don't remember much but you feel funny. Acting character(s) takes note.
11	H7 A pack of wild horses rests nearby. How will you try and catch one? Each character should test individually.	You've got yourself a fresh mount until the end of the Journey. See the Market table.	The horse is irritated and bucks you off. Mark xp and suffer -1 Morale
12	Fip B6: Orientate.	Subtract 1 day from your journey	You are lost. +1 day to this Journey.

TUNDRA**

2d6	EVENT	HIT	MISS
2	M3: The fields of ice seem intimidating. How do you cope?	Acting character(s) takes +1 forward	It's too much and you lose valuable time in dread.
3	B3: Where is that one thing?!	Oh, it was here the whole time.	Acting character(s) chooses 1 item to remove, or suffers -1M forward.
4	H3 Unnatural snowflakes glow eerily. What happens next?	You get through them without incident and Acting character(s) takes +1H forward	Suddenly it's morning and you haven't slept a wink! All characters roll. On a 1-2 become Ensorceled.
5	B4 Snowbeasts appear! What do you do?	You pass them without any real trouble and are able to rest for the day. Acting character(s) takes +1 Mirth.	Their verbal abuse is unexpected and hurtful. All characters -1 Morale.
6	H4: You stop for directions but there seems to be a language barrier between you and the locals. What do you do?	Somehow you manage to communicate and are given directions. You may take -1 Day from your Journey.	You so offend them with your gestures that they swear revenge. Acting character(s) should take note.

REFERENCE

2d6	EVENT	HIT	MISS
7	H4: There in the middle of the ice is a small shrine to Scatha. How do you avoid its bad magic?	The shrine is now a distant memory. Acting character(s) may take advantage forward.	All hail Scatha! Acting character(s) becomes Ensorceled.
8	M5 You find a patch of snowberries! How do you harvest them?	All characters choose: +1 Gear or +1 Morale.	They melt at your touch.
9	B5 The temperature drops. What can you do to keep warm?	You succeed in pushing through the cold, but it's still a bit much. All characters take disadvantage forward.	Acting character(s) rolls. On a 1-2, become Exhausted in Body.
10	M6: A frozen lake offers a bit of ice fishing. Who will crack the ice and fish?	Good catch, buddy! All characters may take +1 Morale or +1 Gear	All characters roll. On a 1-2 fall into the freezing water for -1 Morale
11	H7: A dreadquake shakes body and soul. What do you do?	You make it to safety just in time. All characters take +1 Mirth.	You are caught in the middle of the quake. You survive but the Acting character(s) is shaken and should take note.
12	B5: Orientate	-1 day from this Journey	You are lost. +1 day to this Journey.

Journey's End

Sum up your hits and misses from all your days Adventuring to create a modifier, then roll on the table and add (or subtract) the modifier. May spend gear to boost roll.

1d6	JOURNEY'S END
1	You've never slept so horribly. Choose: you become exhausted in Body or Mind
2	No amount of sleep can help this fatigue: -1 Morale
3	Not too bad, but not a great trip. No effect.
4	The road was not too stressful: +1 Morale or mark XP
5	What a success! Tales will be told of this trek: +1 Mirth
6	A splendid night's sleep! Restore +1d3 morale or mark XP

Arrival

Roll to find out the inn type, its appearance, prestige, specials, and if anything interesting happens when you get there.

2d6	TYPE*
2	Mystics' Lodge
3	Gambling Den
4	Bandit Hideout
5	Postal Stop
6	Intellectual House
7	Plain Old Pub
8	Trading House
9	Rumor Mill
10	Exclusive Club
11	Almshouse or Monastery
12	Artist's Colony

2d6	EXTERIOR APPEARANCE*	2d6	INTERIOR APPEARANCE*
2	A standard looking inn, but with trees for corner posts!	2	Natural appearance: a bar made of vines, toadstool chairs, and so forth
3	Mossy, stacked stones and a pleasing old shingle	3	Magical bookcases everywhere; quiet reading nooks; magical moving book trollies
4	Clean plaster walls accented by red wooden beams.	4	A dark oak saloon, complete with second level balcony
5	Earthen walls, a thatched roof, but a huge stone door that looks like the opening of a vault.	5	Teak wood furniture with stained glass windows
6	Slats of purple wood with pleasant, round windows	6	Black Steel fixtures with mallorn furniture

REFERENCE

2d6	EXTERIOR APPEARANCE*	2d6	INTERIOR APPEARANCE*
7	A standard looking villa, but four stories tall.	7	Iron accents with standard oak tables & chairs
8	This building has two wings made of brick with a big, central courtyard open to the air	8	Brownstone mead hall with a large central fireplace
9	There is only a small shed with a door leading down into the inn.	9	Olive-stained birch panels, cushioned furniture, paintings
10	An open air garden with lush hedges, flowers, and tressled walls between booths	10	Sculpted from a single piece of stone
11	An ethereal tower that seems to flicker between dimensions	11	Black and white: Ivory tables and chairs with an onyx bar
12	A green glass dome.	12	Dragonskin furniture with fire pits everywhere

1d6	PETS*
1	A pack of unhomed cats have taken up refuge in the cellar.
2	The innkeeper has a pet dog about who seems to believe it runs the place.
3	Who let the rather large chameleon in?
4	A friendly pet ocelot is as much a part of the inn as anyone else.
5	One pesky mouse has taken a liking to the place.
6	A past hero boarded their bird here. They got eaten by a dragon and now the bird lives in the rafters.

1d6	PRESTIGE	EFFECT
1	Hovel	This is not as described. Take disadvantage when you roll on the Rest table.
2	Local Favorite	This inn is...acceptable, but bustling. Roll on the Inn Event Table.
3	Well Known	They appreciate your visit and pay extra attention to your needs. +1 on any1 course you choose.
4	Region's Finest	Take advantage when you roll on the table to discover this inn's specialties
5	World Famous	+1 when you Rest here The bustle is a bit much. Roll on the Inn Event's table.
6	Legendary	+1 when you Rest here and clear all conditions Take disadvantage whenever you roll on the Ale, Wine, and Soft Drink table.

REFERENCE

1d6	**SPECIALTIES OF THE HOUSE** *You must choose this course and you take disadvantage when you roll to test*
1	The **ale** is experimental
2	The **wine** course will be...different.
3	All of the **soft drinks** are brought in from outside, so you know what that means.
4	The **aperitif** is what some call "nontraditional."
5	The **Entree** uses an exotic ingredient.
6	They say the **desserts** here have been cursed by the Lady of the Southlands.

1d6	**ARRIVAL EVENT****
1	It is busier than expected. Roll 1d6. On a 1-2 the standing is unbearable. -1 Morale
2	There's something odd happening. Roll on the Events table.
3	A Society rival is here to **Interfere**. Describe them. Roll on the Interference table immediately.
4	All is calm and you are seen to right away. Proceed with +1 forward.
5	A peddler is here. You may roll on the Market table if you wish.
6	The mood is infectiously cheerful! Take +1 Mirth.

THE BROKEN CASK SOCIETY

1d6	INTERFERENCE
1	They are chatting you up incessantly ands spoiling your mood. Take disadvantage forward.
2	They are very suspicious. Pick one course during the feast. During that course roll and on a 1-2 become poisoned.
3	They give you some disturbing news. What is it that has you so upset? Take disadvantage when you **rest** here.
4	They, surprisingly, act in a true spirit of camaraderie. Cheers! +1 Mirth.
5	The conversation leaves you feeling better. Take +1 forward.
6	Something else is going on. Roll on the Inn Event Table.

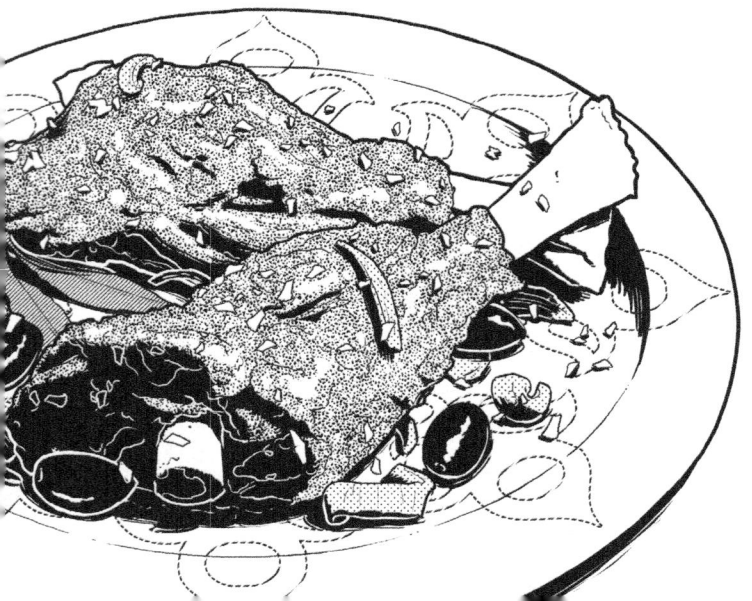

Inn Event Table

2d6	INN EVENT TABLE
2	Flip B4 - A full on tavern brawl has broken out! What do you do? All characters must test individually. **Hit:** You have survived with nary a scratch and are offered compensation! Choose one course when you Feast; hit automatically on that course. **Miss:** The inn is pretty well smashed up and so are you. Mark XP and choose: -1d6 Morale or become Sick from the beatdown.
3	M3 - There appears to be a small kitchen fire. How can you help? **Hit:** The fire is put out with minimal damage and the innkeeper offers you an upgraded room. Take +1 when you roll on the Rest table. **Miss:** Luckily a Society rival was there to fix things in your stead. How embarrassing. Take note.
4	H4 - Mischievous Witches are causing a scene and blasting magic all over. What do you do? **Hit:** Whatever you did, it worked, and they've offered a protective spell. Take +1 Morale or +1 Mirth instead. **Miss:** Oh dear, I think you've been struck. Mark XP. Roll 1d6. On a 1-2 something terrible has happened. What is it? Skip the Feast and go straight to Rest.
5	M3 - Some festival has just occurred and the inn is being flooded with guests. How will you help ensure you are not interrupted? **Hit:** The revelers make space and you feel a newfound confidence. Take +1 forward. **Miss:** The staff is swamped and distracted. When you Feast, choose 1 course: automatically treat that course as a missed roll.

Table continues on next page.

6	H4 - The bard just broke a string. This is awkward. What do you do? **Hit:** The situation is amended and they teach you a new song! What is it? Take note. **Miss:** The evening's entertainment is over. Mark XP and take disadvantage forward.
7	B5 - An adventurer stands and begins sharing their latest successes quite loudly and quite annoyingly. What do you do? **Hit:** The rest of the room is grateful and buy you a round. Choose: +1H forward or automatically hit the next beverage course. **Miss:** The adventurer does not take kindly to your interference! Test B3. On a miss they slug you for -1Morale. On a hit Mark XP.
8	H5 - Some rowdy singing has broken out. It's cheerful...but distracting. What do you do? **Hit:** The singing subsides and you feel a bit more pleasant. Take advantage forward. **Miss:** Now it's just annoying. Take disadvantage forward.
9	M6 A riddle game breaks out! How do you defend yourself? **Hit:** As the riddle champ you may take +1 Mirth. **Miss:** The last riddle truly confounds you and you cannot get it out of your mind. Mark XP and take note.
10	B6 The Purple Burglar sneaks about, picking pockets. How aware are you? **Hit:** You catch them in the act! Roll on the rare items table to claim your prize. **Miss:** Pilfered! Remove one item *or* -1 Gear.
11	H7 - A portal seems to have opened up... **Hit:** The portal closes and you are the heroes of the night. Improve now. **Miss:** Mark 2 XP and end the session.
12	All is quiet and pleasing. Choose: +1 Mirth or mark XP.

REFERENCE

Feast

Choose any combination of six drink courses and meal courses (one must be the Special). Roll d66 on one table at a time. After each course is discovered, all players test to find out if they enjoy it or not.

On a hit mark Mirth. On a miss you do not enjoy it! Mark Xp and then roll on the React table to see what happens.

d66	ALES
11	B2 Badger Bock
12	M2 Bluebark Porter
13	H2 Melon Rind Ale
14	B2 Born Well Brown
15	M2 Elephant Beer
16	H2 Brokenose Lager
21	B2 Snowberry Mead
22	M2 Fairy Sweat White Ale
23	H2 Antler's Ale
24	Flip B3 Plain Ol Pint
25	M3 Ogre's Breath Wheat
26	H3 Shinsong River Wheat
31	B2 Darkstone Dunkel
32	M2 Lager of Ten Downs
33	H2 Proudfoot Pale Ale
34	B3 Lambic of MacGorilla
35	M4 Midnight Sun Cider
36	H4 Ternary Mead
41	B4 Goldtooth Golden Ale

Table continues on next page.

42	M3 Withered Berry Brew
43	H3 Ale's Well as Ends Better
44	B5 Silverfroth
45	M5 Sunrose Ruby Red Ale
46	H5 Farmer Arable's Saison
51	B4 Partridge Berry Pilsner
52	M4 Stout & About
53	H4 Barley Breathing
54	B6 White Sierra Ale
55	M5 Ghastly Ghoul Grog
56	M6 Wizard's Biscuit
61	H6 Praline Pilsner
62	B5 Hogger's Hobnogger Pilsner
63	M6 Stout Imperial Ale
64	H7 Dragonfire Double Bock
65	B7 Lickspittle
66	M7 Hardy Mulberry Mead

d66	**WINES**
11	B2 Mudhoney Noir
12	M2 Breakneck's Malbec
13	H2 Grasshopper Blend
14	B2 Black Wine
15	M2 Candlewax
16	H2 Lamp Wine
21	B2 Thirteen Mirages White Blend
22	M2 Sparkling Snow Wine

REFERENCE

23	H2 Pookah Riesling
24	B3 Turf
25	M3 Thalki's Blood
26	H3 Medusa Merlot
31	B2 Sparkling Herbshine
32	M2 Stormy Cabernet
33	H2 Zinfandel of Drottnar
34	B3 Chianti of Plaitbeard
35	M4 Gormonberry Sherry
36	H4 Great Sulfur Chardonnay
41	B4 The Sultan's Sultana
42	M3 White Chocolate Grenache
43	H3 Intemperate Tempranillo
44	B5 Redpeckle Rosé
45	Flip M5 Pelican Pecan Blend
46	H5 Cabernet of Chaotic Neutral
51	B4 Tiefling Tempranillo
52	M4 Old Winyards
53	H4 Tulaberry Wine
54	B6- Gamay of Barghest Heart
55	M5 White Speckled Rose
56	M6 Muskrat Muscato
61	H6 Hard to Port
62	B5 The Dark Lord's Dark Blend
63	M6 Blasted Tulip Noir
64	H7 Twin Hype Merlot
65	B7 Rosé of the Dungeon Shaker
66	M7 Zero Point Zero Blend

d66	SOFT DRINKS
11	B2 Soft Root Cider
12	M2 Birch Beer
13	H2 Ginger Ale
14	B2 Sparkling Cactus Water
15	M2 Heavy Roast Coffee
16	H2 Kvass
21	B2 Potion of Power Attack (it's actually just prune juice)
22	M2 Boba Tea
23	H2 Orange Frappe
24	B3 Fey Mixed Tea
25	M3 Pomegranate Molasses
26	H3 Red Rhino Tea
31	B2 Spring Seltzer
32	M2 Sweetgum Lassi
33	H2 Dark Mint Coffee
34	B3 Mermaid Cola
35	M4 Frostheart Syrup
36	H4 Black Tea
41	B4 Prune Juice
42	M3 Mixed Berry Soft Cider
43	H3 Coffee with Auroch's Milk
44	B5 Chai
45	M5 Sujeonggwa Cinnamon
46	H5 Dragon Fruit Soda
51	B4 Mungo's Mango Milk
52	M4 Old Maud's Ginger Tea
53	H4 Monk's Milktea

REFERENCE

54	B6 Darjeeling
55	H6 Queen of the Southlands Tea
56	M6 Gurgling Yerba Mate
61	H6 Atole of Angmar
62	B5 Spring Villager Blend Tea
63	M6 Sparkling Mugwort Soda
64	H7 Twigstem Tea
65	B7 Peppermint Lassi
66	M7 Fox Breath Blend Coffee

d66	APERITIF
11	B2 Barley Bread & Butter
12	M2 Soup D'Jour (it's the soup of the day)
13	H2 Fairy Cheese Voulevant
14	B2 Gammer Bogg's Vegetable Medley
15	M2 Mini Mince Tarts
16	H2 Fish Stuffed Cabbage Roll
21	B2 Ploughman's Lunch
22	M2 Kibbe bi Lahim
23	Flip H2 Fried Beetroot Sticks
24	B3 Spring Onion Omelet
25	M3 Barley Soup for Brigands
26	H3 Harpy Cakes
31	B2 Black & White Pudding
32	M2 Kunnia Sandwich
33	H2 Carbuncle Root Salad with Vinaigrette
34	B3 Cave Carrot Potage with Herbs

Table continues on next page.

35	M4 Mixed Fruit Pasty
36	H4 Lycanthrope Ichor Surprise
41	B4 Frostbite Cashew Dip with Watercress
42	M3 Melted Gruyere Sarnie
43	H3 Green Pea Soup with Cracklin'
44	B5 Farmer's Bamboo Salad with Tahini
45	M5 Vicious Vichyssoise
46	H5 Grain, Okra, and Curry Mash
51	B4 Darkvision Dainties
52	M4 Hopped Cream of Carrot Soup
53	H4 Fried Parsnip Bits with Glow worm ice
54	B6 Mullet & Leek Turnover
55	H6 Fried Bean Patties
56	M6 Ginger Salad
61	H6 Ork's Fire Snack Mix
62	B5 Warm Rhubarb Stew
63	M6 Orkish Pull-apart Bread
64	H7 Bloomin' Onion
65	B7 Creamed Lentil Spread on Barley Bread
66	M7 Minced Frog's Tongue Soup

d66	ENTREE
11	B2 Frog-in-the-hole
12	M2 Gareth's Garlic Noodles
13	H2 Cherub Leaf Porridge
14	B2 Roast Duck with Bilberry Reduction
15	M2 Roast Vegetables Wraps with Hydra Sauce
16	H2 Pan-seared Pike stuffed with Rose Buds

REFERENCE

21	B2 Rack of Lamb with Mint Chutney
22	M2 Kraken's Ink Ziti
23	H2 Ogrin Liver Masala
24	B3 Buttered Turmeric Roots
25	M3 Ironfold Ham with Brie rolls
26	H3 Bubble & Squeak
31	Flip B2 Sweet Jackalope Barbecue
32	M2 Flank Steak of Quintessence
33	H2 Sausage and Mash
34	B3 Beef Turnover with Cucumber Salt
35	M4 Mushroom Pie with Saffron
36	H4 Sno Og Granskog (we don't know what it is either)
41	B4 Seitanic Veggie Pie
42	M3 Calf's Brain Aspic
43	H3 Fava-stuffed Waybread
44	B5 Pit-roasted Quilboar
45	M5 Wild Salamander in a Blanket
46	H5 Pear Glazed Bean Steak
51	B4 Chicken Fried Chicken Steak with Chicken
52	M4 Dragonscale Charcuterie Plate
53	H4 Smoked Dwarf Beard Fowl
54	B6 Pan-seared Sphinx Livers with Parsley
55	H6 Gaffers Rare Dumplings
56	M6 Holy Snapper in a Redcap Demi-glace
61	H6 Fried Chickpea Bites of Knowledge
62	B5 Veggie Burger of the Thunderwave
63	M6 Oxtail Soup with Mint
64	H7 Bean, Leak, & Sunchoke Casserole
65	B7 Faerie Fire Hotpot
66	M7 Truffle Butter Buckbeak Wings

d66	DESSERT
11	B2 Sorbet. Just sorbet.
12	M2 Sweetbread Pudding
13	H2 Uncle Nessus' Chocolate Creme
14	B2 Lavender Cake with Syrup
15	M2 Elephant Ear Pastry
16	H2 Tiny's Treacle
21	B2 Fresh Pitaya Scones
22	M2 Orris Root Tart
23	H2 Snakeroot Biscuits
24	B3 Coriander Apple Pie with Coffee
25	M3 Starfish Gelatin with Pineberries
26	H3 Citrus Shaved Ice of Strength
31	B2 Furrier's Fine Flan
32	M2 Poison Oak Custard
33	H2 Cobwebbed Layer Cake
34	B3 Mugwort Iced Tart
35	M4 Weald-bride Meringue
36	H4 Misty Zephyr Brownies
41	B4 Barkskin Chocolate Bark
42	M3 Double Sweet Peony Traybake
43	H3 Orange Sugar Fig Cake
44	B5 Sabretooth Madeleines
45	M5 Chanterelle Crumble
46	H5 Perrywinkle Yule Log
51	B4 Dying Breath Sponge
52	M4 Three Milk Meringue
53	H4 Macadamia Cookies of Courage

54	B6 Worm Caviar with Shaved Sugarcane
55	H6 Lupine Sorbet
56	M6 Almond Shell Pastry
61	H6 Syrup-soaked Valerian Root Buns
62	Flip B5 Acai Drop Ice
63	M6 Cave Bat Pie
64	H7 Huckleberry Scones of Fleetness
65	B7 Dragonfruit Mochi
66	M7 White Cake

React Table

When you miss a course, roll on the table below to find out what's happened.

1d6	REACTION
1	It's just bad. -1 Morale
2	It's not sitting quite right. Roll. On a 1-2 take -1 Morale.
3	Okay, it's really bad. Become poisoned.
4	Someone has recognized you at exactly the wrong time. Roll on the Interference table.
5	Something is distracting you from this course. Roll on the Inn Events table.
6	You manage to stomach it and press on.

Rest

Double check for modifiers then roll on the rest table.

1d6	REST
1	Something at the inn is disturbing your sleep. Roll on the Inn Event table and test. Ignore the consequences. Instead, on a hit take +1 Morale; on a miss -1 Morale.
2	-1 Morale
3	+1 Morale or mark XP
4	You rest well enough! +1d3 Morale or +1 Mirth
5	Comfy. +1d6 Morale or +1 Mirth
6	A splendid night's sleep! Restore all Morale and choose: +1 Journey forward or clear a condition.

Epilogue

If you wish, when you end your session, roll to find out how this story ends for your character.

1d6	EPILOGUE*
1	You publish your adventures in the Society newsletter. How is it received?
2	You offer advice to the last innkeeper, increasing their business and earning you free board whenever your travels take you there. What was it?
3	You return with gifts for your loved ones. What happens?
4	You discover something amazing on your return journey. What is it?
5	Tales of your journey inspire fresh recruits for the Society. How do you know them?
6	Your journeys inspire you to create a new recipe. What is it?

Market Table

1d6	MARKET TABLE
1	You are able to procure a weapon! You may not know what to do with this thing, but it'll help keep you safe. Describe it or roll on the weapons table below. *Take +1 on any test involving any attack (monsters, brigands, etc)
2	Rations, sleep sacks, a walking stick, they've got it all! +1 Gear
3	A gift for the next innkeeper! What is it? Take advantage forward on the Arrival table.
4	It's that one book you've been looking for...which one was that, again? Spend to choose: +1 XP or +1 Mirth
5	This digestive cordial will help you overcome any fits of gastrointestinal distress. Spend it to remove poisoned or sick condition.
6	Roll on the rare items table.

1d6	DESCRIPTOR*	WEAPONS
1	Pasta	Flail
2	Moosey	Sword
3	Doomsong	Magic Scroll
4	Flatulent	Two-handed Ax
5	Administerial	Dirk
6	Pointy	Crossbow

1d6	RARE ITEMS
1	This vendor has mounts available on the cheap! Describe it or roll on the fauna table. Take +1 Adventure ongoing or spend to remove one day from a Journey (affects you only; not your party).
2	Stupid Uncle Egg's Good Time Snake Oil can be spent to clear all conditions.
3	Map Spend to take advantage on any Adventure roll, either on the table or when you test
4	Hate Cloak Next time you would roll on the Interference table, spend to cancel the roll (before you make the roll, of course)
5	Enchanted Tankard Spend to flip when you test on any beverage course then it vanishes..
6	Magical Familiar Describe your familiar. Spend to automatically hit any test on which they may be able to help you.

1d6	FAUNA TABLE
1	Lavender Oxen
2	Horse
3	Hyppogriffs
4	Fire Toads
5	Giant Bats
6	Battle Goats

1d6	SETTLEMENT TABLE
1	A rustic tent city
2	A dusty old town
3	A country village
4	A charming hamlet
5	A large stone city
6	A regal elvish city

Random Character Traits

d66	NAME	d66	TITLE
11	Rocso	11	Sunborn
12	Waldorf	12	Of the Coastlands
13	Dirn	13	The Venomous
14	Odo	14	Dourhand
15	Kelfi	15	Clear-eye
16	Rudgren	16	The Drunken
21	Folen	21	Steeltruss
22	Hagas	22	Goldbrow
23	Lark	23	Skyway
24	Takanos	24	Smith
25	Bessarion	25	The Imposter
26	Walaran	26	Moonshield
31	Gorge	31	Stonemover

Table continues on next page.

32	Galkos	32	Silvertongue
33	Usi	33	Boatman
34	Parn	34	Harvestwing
35	Kalimetos	35	Of the Ten Winds
36	Taja	36	The Banished
41	Faff	41	The Slowcoach
42	Autumo	42	The Laureled
43	Doro	43	Redleaf
44	Skrymer	44	Trollhorn
45	Ella	45	Far-goer
46	Beravor	46	Wolftooth
51	Porphyrios	51	The Swift
52	Ezri	52	Brownsleeves
53	Gram	53	The Borrower
54	Lauren	54	Of the Blackwold
55	Kendall	55	The Knight
56	Kenlin	56	The Bride
61	Vreth	61	Wintermind
62	Grutle	62	Necrobutcher
63	Xenia	63	The Grand
64	Davion	64	Starflight
65	Adassa	65	Of the Isles
66	Nico	66	One-eye

REFERENCE

2d6	HERITAGE
2	Dragonkin
3	Half-ork
4	Dwarf
5	Elf
6	Halfling
7	Human
8	Half-elf
9	Satyr
10	Skin-changer
11	Goblin
12	Troll

2d6	QUIRKS
2	They seem to genuinely be unable to stop talking.
3	For some reason or other they always feel the need to gamble.
4	They are compulsive about one thing in particular
5	They are allergic to a certain animal's fur, of which you've got some on you.
6	They are agreeable until the topic of distilling comes up.
7	They have an extremely annoying laugh.
8	Their accent is off-putting. Why?
9	They appear to be nocturnal.
10	They are in a great amount of debt. To who?
11	They have great skill in fixing machinery and they love to talk about it.
12	They have a phobia of what?

BACKERS LIST

- Adam Cousino
- Adam Criblez
- Addie, Avie, and Livia Bogdan
- Adrià Prat
- Akos Malindovszky
- Al Gonzalez
- Alan Hatcher
- Alana Wolfgang-Duran
- Alex T.
- Alissa
- Allan Bray
- Amanda
- Anders Lund
- André Varela
- Andrew C Stackhouse
- Andy Buell
- Andy O'Hara
- Andy Yeoh
- Anne O'Nymous
- Anonymous
- Anubis
- Austen Sprake
- Avri
- Axel Schaupp
- Bat Martin-McCall
- BE Holt
- Bellamy Maleiß
- Ben Mandall
- Bethanie
- Bjorn
- Blitzbuff
- Blunder Woman
- Bobkytten
- Bonnie Mann
- Boris
- BrawnyFanta
- Brett Moses
- Brian Griffin
- Bridgette Findley
- brothgar
- Bruce Baugh
- Bryan Gago

Bun Perez
C & A Lyons
Captain Ogre
Carinn Seabolt
Carl Black
Carson Brooks
Cassi Rae
Catastrophi
Chad Andrew Bale
Charles Schmidt
Charlotte Heilling
ChrisG
Christopher Rivera
Christopher Spivak
ChubbyCupcakez
Cid Carbano
Cindy Si Tou
Cire4ever
CJ Graham
Clutterbooke
CMCF
Cody "Crazy" Stump
Cody Schlitter
ColinandBlakesFodir Sison
Cornell Daly
Dan Suptic
DanB
Daniel Garding
Darren Davis
David Hayes

David Stephenson
David W. Bauer
David W. Marshall
Davide Birolini
Deborah Gard
Dillon Trelawny
DocChronos
DonkeyJay
Dorien S
Douglas A Christy
Drewseph McKlannington Moody Cask Builder
E. Pentico
E.Contesse
Ed McCutchan
Eliot B. Chenowith
Elizabeth Cook
Elizabeth Davis
Emily Brooks
Emily L
Endre Enyedy
Eric Atkinson
Eric Buetikofer
Eric Garlow
Erika Mullineaux
Erin J. Giannelli
Eversong
EWC
Fred Herman
Frederick Paepke

BACKERS LIST

Friendly Local Game Pod
Gareth J. Coster
Gary Arnold
Gavin "Moose" Evans
Gianluca Casu
GregorGB
Griffin D. Morgan
Gutom na Dragon at ang kanyang maliit na Manok
Hans Messersmith
Harley Rayne
Harold Dean Darby II
Hawk
Heptalemma
Heracynn Raine
HonestJon311
Hudson Phillips
Il Giova della Locanda Shakespiriana per Moschettieri
ineedtosleep
Isaiah J
Its_Tea
J Bohlmann
J, Whitham
Jacob Crosby
Jacob N Walker
James Ash
James Torr
Jan Časta
Jared Reiman
Jason Lindner
Jason M Brown
Jason Martin
Jasper
Jay chin
Jay Esse H
Jeff Eppenbach
Jeff Schultz
Jeff Wilms
Jennifer 'Tirima' Parker
Jeremy Riel
Jess M
Jody Whittle
Joel Buntin
Jonathan Snavely
Josh Ivanov
Joshua Barry
Joshua Connor
Joshua Roots
JR the Frog
Julien "Spook" Gomez
Justin Alexander Dorsey
Justin McCormick
Justin Porter
Justin Tucker
Kari Dayton
Kat
Kat L.
Kate Luginbuhl
Kelley Carter

THE BROKEN CASK SOCIETY

Kelly Brown
Kelly L M Wardle
Kevin M. Gallagher, Jr.
Kimberly Moler
Kris Leeke
Kristoffer "Illern" Holmén
Lachlan Jones
Laura Lea Davidson
Lauren Skye Sila
Leighton
Len C
Leo Bullimore
Liam Montier
Lilly Ibelo
Lina B.
Lisa Hunt
Lisa Padol
Louis Roseguo
LoveDruid
Lukas Feinweber
Luke Woods
MacDhomnuill Games
Maciej "Avril" Matuszewski
Mac-Mac
Manuel Dornbusch
Mao & Jon Wildmane
Mark Clark Jr
Martin Pinkerton
Martin Prucha
Matt Bohnhoff

Matthew Tucker
Max Lawson
Melissa Cruz-Campbell
Michael Blackwell
Michael Schwartz
Michelle Katz
Mike "Lochen" P
Mike Carlson
Mike Dubost
Mike Field
Mike Mendoza
Mimi
Min Yong Ro
Mitch Kidder
Morandia
Mox, a Kobold Chef
MUZAQ
Myridian
Natasha Ence
Nathan D. Clark
Nathan Early
Nathan Hostetter
Neal T
Neil Garland
Nick Gould
Nick Wild
Niel Bornstein
Nocturne
Nojus Š.
NonaKnowsGames

BACKERS LIST

Olavi Turunen
Olna Jenn Smith
OO
Paul Boquet
Paul R. Smith
Peregrine F.
Peter T
Philip Wilde
Please dont
Raechel S.
Ransom Meltzer
Raúl Polo Molina
Rebecca K
Redacted & Kaal – Cool People Like Us
Renee Bargy-Smith
Rhiannon Plessman
Richard Joyce
Robert De Luna
Robin Powell
Robin Tapfield
Ronald Schachtner
Ross Salerno
Ruth Gibbs
Ryan Coombes
Ryan Lenig
Sandy Wright
Sarah Kilsch
Sarah Liberman
Sean E Pierce
Sebastian
Sebastian Hennicke
Shane Zuspan
Shaun S
Shedvin
Shelby D. White
Shiloh Strawn
Sierra Trees-Turner
Skye Nathaniel Schiefer
"Slàinte Mhath" Jean Rolfe
Snowman
sonoghen
spacewiz
Stacy Weaver
Steady Prism
Steffen Janßen
Stephen Nichols
Steven Barrett
Steven Byrd
T.J. Yarcia
Taz da Spaz
Team Watusi
Tera Boster
Thane & Rafe Dube
The Dungeon Dive
The Eye of Xegim
The Gluttonous Geek
The Laughing Alchemist
Theodore C Barry
Tim Ellis

THE BROKEN CASK SOCIETY

Tim W

Tom Cohen

Tommy Chu

Tonkinese

Travis Agaman

Trip Space-Parasite

two pints of ale and
    a scotch egg

Tyler M

TyWuNon

Vancat

Victor Haerinck Jr.

Walter Koegel

Will Darquehope

William Miller

Xevi

Y. K. Lee

Zelroc

Printed in Great Britain
by Amazon